Publisher's note: This is another of Martin
Archer's exciting and action packed novels in
The Company of Archers saga about an
Englishman who rose to become the captain of
what was left of a company of crusading English
archers – and what happened to him and his men
after he led the survivors of his company back to
the dangerous and brutal land of medieval
England. The first book in this saga is entitled
The Archers.

PREFACE

Taking a train full of currency or capturing a Spanish treasure ship is nothing compared to the greatest thefts in history—when the captain of a company of English archers and his men systematically stole the entire treasury and religious relics of the world's greatest and richest empire and escaped to Cornwall with chests and chests of gold and priceless relics. This is part of the on-going story of how it all began and what happened when he tried to turn the relics into coins for himself and his men. Today's men would have done quite well in medieval times. *The Company of English Archers.*

Book Three
The Archers Return
Chapter One

It was mid-April and the channel storms had subsided
when I gave my son and my priestly brother a final big
hug and issued the order for our galleys and cogs to cast
off and head down the Fowey and out into the channel.
We were going to make a dash to the coast of France
before the weather changes again.

It was quite a fleet we'd put together—we were
sailing for the Holy Land with twelve of our fourteen
Cornwall-based galleys and both of our large cargo-
carrying, single-masted cogs going out as pirate-takers.
They were carrying just over one thousand of the sailors
and archers we'd recruited and trained since we left the
Holy Land a year ago.

Almost every archer in our company was in the
fleet. Only a handful of the veterans needed to train our
new apprentice archers were being left behind in
Cornwall. We were bound for the Mediterranean to once
again earn our bread carrying Christian and Jewish

refugees to safety and taking Moorish prizes.

My basic plan was quite simple as all good plans must be—dash across the channel to France when the weather is good and then turn right and follow the French and Portuguese coasts to a rendezvous at Lisbon, and then another at the port of Palma on the Island of Mallorca.

From Palma we'd sail on to Crete where we'd rendezvous again. And from Crete, we'd sail and row our way to Malta; perhaps to even set up some sort of a permanent base on the island if its ruler, our old pirate friend, Brindisi, would allow us to do so.

Then it would be on to Cyprus to join the galleys and cogs we already have in the Holy Land. It was the reverse of the route we followed last year to get what was left of our original company of archers back to England.

If all went exactly according to my plan, which wasn't at all likely if the past is any guide, our galleys would hug the coast and pick up water along the way at the little villages that are inevitably located at the mouth of the smaller rivers and streams running into the sea.

The village people would often not be friendly and almost always hard to understand because they speak so many strange dialects, particularly when we reach that part of the Spanish coast where the villagers are mostly heathen Moslems—but no matter how they pray, there was little they could do to stop our war galleys from gathering water when we anchor at a river's mouth and begin dipping in our leather buckets.

Our two cogs were carrying more water skins and

water barrels than the galleys so they'd be able to travel farther out and stop less frequently. Even so, they'd tend to follow as close to the coast as possible in an effort to attract pirates—because they were going out as pirate-takers and the Moorish pirate galleys tend to stay close to shore so they can be pulled ashore on dry land if a storm approaches.

Palma should once again be interesting—and, as usual, a bit dicey because it was a Moorish port with a Moslem ruler where the Christians from Genoa and Pisa have concessions.

So shall we one day, I hope. Have our own concessions in Palma, I mean.

My priestly brother and I had learnt a lot from all the mistakes we made getting the survivors of our company of archers back to England from King Richard's crusade. That's why each and every galley and cog I was leading out to Cyprus and the Holy Land ports was sailing with at least two or three experienced pilots, a full crew of sailors, and highly trained archers equipped with longbows and long-handled bladed pikes, and as many water skins and water barrels as it could carry in addition to its crew and supplies.

On the other hand, some things won't be changed. Both of our cogs will be going out as pirate bait with their archers and swordsmen hidden until a Moorish pirate galley comes alongside and grapples them to hold them tight whilst the pirates board.

Hopefully, the pirates will do so, board I mean, thinking they are about to take an unarmed cargo cog and will soon have the cog and its cargo and its crew as slaves to sell.

Slaves taken by the Moslems are important to the Moslems' "Grand Caliph" or whatever their pope is calling himself these days. Selling them is how he was getting the coins he was using to pay for his war in Spain against the Christians of Castile and Leon.

Anyhow, that's what my brother Thomas says and he's usually right, being as he is so well read and such from reading all nine books at the monastery before he left for an archer and took me crusading with him—and damn near got us both killed.

Pirate galleys are very much like ours; they tend to stay to closer in to shore so they can take on water and run up into the local streams and harbours for shelter when there is a storm at sea. They also like to throw grappling irons on to innocent-appearing cargo cogs such as ours and swarm aboard to take the cogs as prizes and their sailors as slaves.

When a pirate galley comes alongside and its crew begins to board, our cogs' sailors will throw their own grapples to hold the pirate galley even tighter so it can't get away. That's when our cogs' real cargos, an entire company of English archers and other fighting men—our marine archers as we've come to sometimes call those of our men who've been learnt to fight both on land and on the sea—will charge out from the cogs' deck castles and holds where they've been hiding and sweep the surprised and outnumbered pirates into the sea.

At least, that was one of the things my priestly

brother, Thomas, and I intend for our cogs to do on their return voyage to the Holy Land. If it works, and it certainly has in the past, we'll be able to take some pirate galleys as prizes and add them to those we are already using to carry pilgrims to the Holy Land—and then use them again to rescue the pilgrims when they become refugees and are willing to pay good coins to get away from the heathen Saracens.

Our archer-carrying cogs are quite special. There are a lot of galleys crewed by heathen pirates everywhere in the Mediterranean, and with a little luck, our pirate-taking cogs will attract some of them before we reach Palma.

What Thomas and I haven't shared with any of our men is what I plan to have our galleys do after we reach Palma. It's a good plan and will no doubt work perfectly as all battle plans do in their makers' minds—until the fighting actually starts and everything changes.

****** *William*

I was sailing on my lucky galley—the big one with forty-four oars on each side that carried George and me and our coin chests safely all the way back to England. Harold is once again the galley's sergeant captain and the master sergeant over all the sergeant captains commanding our galleys and cogs. He is by far the best galley captain we've got, even if he can't scribe or gobble in church talk.

Young Peter, the fast-thinking archer from the battle at Launceston, is coming with me as my helper and fetcher. I was initially going to leave Peter at Launceston to be second to Martin, the veteran archer who is steady but slow. In the end, I changed my mind and left a defrocked Italian priest, Angelo Priestly, to assist Martin who is Launceston's constable—because Martin doesn't know how to read and Thomas likes to send scribed messages.

Thomas found the ex-priest and vouched for his honesty and ability to scribe and sum. It was obviously something personal that got him thrown out of the church or caused him to run. Whatever it was, Thomas seemed quite sympathetic and willing to ignore it.

Our Palma-bound galley and cogs will try to stick together for as long as possible by hanging candle lanterns on our masts at night. It'll be good practise for what we are going to try to do after we leave Palma. Sooner or later, of course, we'll be separated when the lanterns are lost from sight or the weather changes and drives us apart. Then each galley would sail to Palma on its own.

****** *William*

Sooner came fairly quickly. We were pretty much able to stay together until we left Lisbon. But within hours of rowing out of Lisbon's great harbour, a big storm scattered us and it was every galley and cog for itself. Each was alone as it headed towards Gibraltar and the entrance to the Mediterranean—and the Moorish pirate galleys we hoped to find on our way to Cyprus.

The seas were high and the storm's gusting winds

were blowing towards shore. That wasn't much of a problem for our galleys because they can row to keep ourselves offshore. It was a big problem, however, for the cogs—their crews had to constantly shift their sails about to keep from getting blown into the surf and rocks.

What was a big problem for the galleys was the cold sea water that constantly leaks through their wooden hulls and sometimes comes in over the bows in rough weather because they sit so low to the water. We were, as the sailors like to say, all too often freezing our wet arses off and having to constantly bail like galley slaves with our leather buckets.

Also, although there wasn't anything I could do about it, I was increasingly worried about our two cogs. The wind was all wrong for them and they didn't have oars to row themselves to safety if they got blown towards a dangerous shore.

It's hard to believe, I know, but it's true—the wind can actually blow against a cog's mast and the side of the cog's hull sticking up out of the water and they act as sails. That's what blew Richard's future queen and his sister ashore on Cyprus all those years ago and caused us to go there with him to fight to rescue them instead of going straight for the Holy Land and Jerusalem.

Everyone including me and Harold bailed and rowed in the storm for almost two cold and exhausting days. Then the weather suddenly cleared up, and we passed Gibraltar Castle running before the wind with our leather sail up on our galley's stubby little mast and periodically rowing once our rowers' arms got enough rest to recover their strength.

The storm really did us in, at least it did for me—and I've got an archer's strong arms, so I can only imagine how the sailors and men-at-arms felt who'd never pulled a bow in practice or for real.

****** *William*

To everyone's surprise, we were not alone as we came out of the storm and into the clear weather beyond it.

One of our cogs, the one with the big patch on its sail captained by Albert the archer sergeant from Devon, came up on us fast as we both came out of the storm at the same time—so fast because of the favourable winds coming from the storm, that we had to row hard to keep up so we could talk as we entered the narrows and passed the big Gibraltar rock with the huge Moorish castle on its peak.

I wonder why are there no Moorish galleys here at the entrance to collect tolls and taxes and such? We'd have them here if we could take the rock. Hmm.

Harold managed to keep Albert Devon's cog in sight, and we were able to reach the harbour at Palma together two days later. To my absolute delight, our other cog was already at anchor in the harbour and four of our galleys were moored to the quay.

There were happy hails and waves all around as we entered the harbour and dropped our anchors. Within minutes, dinghies were rowing towards us to report in and share the latest news.

******

Palma is on coast of Mallorca Island. It's a beautiful city and under the nominal control of some Moors from a tribe called "Berburs" or something like that.

What's good for us, and the reason we've put in here for water and to re-form our fleet so that we can sail out together, is that the Moslems are in the midst of another of their long-running and bloody civil wars—and Mallorca's Berbur ruler is a deadly enemy of the Moslem Caliph who rules Tunis and Algiers on the other side of the Mediterranean.

The fighting between the Moslems may be bad for the local people and merchants of Palma, but it was good for us because the local heathens were keen to tell us everything they could about their equally heathen enemies on the other side of the sea—and they had a lot to tell us that might be useful.

Whether what they tell us will be useful is always uncertain, but it certainly beats nothing. Information about your enemies is always important, isn't it?

All and all, as we knew from our last visit, Palma was apparently a fairly civilised place with many Christians and Jews living on the island as farmers and merchants. Genoa and Pisa have had commercial establishments here for many years.

The tavern and the two alehouses next to the quay weren't bad either, just smoky when it got cold at night and their warming fires were lit. The tavern, in particular, has great bread and cheese even though the girls smell bad.

We'd come back to Palma again to refresh our supplies and get information about the Moorish pirates because we didn't have any problems when we called in here in the past—both when we rendezvoused here last year on our way to England and again when our galleys stopped here in September on their way back to Cyprus from England.

Once again, it seemed to be the case, them being friendly, I mean. Indeed, the local Moslems said they were pleased that we'd given the Tunisians such a good poke in the eye last year. At least, that's the story we got from the local merchants both when we called in here last year and on this visit as well.

The Genoan and Pisan merchants were another matter entirely. They were Christians and very much like the island's Jewish and Moslem merchants and merchants everywhere—all smiles and happy enough to take our coins in the market place and pay us to carry their cargos.

On the other hand, according to several of the Jewish merchants, however, the Genoans and Pisans were not at all happy to see us in Palma once again. They knew about our concession and trading posts on Cyprus and elsewhere; they feared we'd come here and set up to be their competitors for the Christian trade.

And, of course, they're right to be worrying about us because someday Thomas and I will indeed be establishing a shipping post here if our plan succeeds.

Unfortunately, the day for us to establish a post here would appear to be a long way off—so we'll do as we've done before and go out of our way to convince the local Christians and everyone else that we are friendly and merely passing through our way to the Holy Land to earn more coins carrying refugees and pilgrims.

Of course, we were acting friendly—it isn't good for trade to scatter shite where you walk and we almost certainly will want to stop here again as we come and go between Cornwall and Cyprus. Even so, the local Christians didn't trust us and I didn't trust them, and rightly so.

I also didn't trust the local Moslem ruler because he's a Moslem. It's well known that they'll change sides in an instant and cut off your head if one of their priests tells them that's what God wants or they start listening to one of their wives or mistresses. They're very much like our Christian kings and popes, aren't they?

If we ever come here permanently, we'll probably have to take over the whole island and get rid of all the Moslems. Unfortunately, we're still a long way off from being strong enough to do it. Besides, we have other more important bread to bake.

****** *William*

"It's good to see everyone again," I told our captain sergeants as they assembled on the deck of Harold's galley to report to me and him. When all the captains in the harbour finished climbing on board, I gathered them around me on the deck to tell them the plan.

But I'm only going to tell them a small part of it and I do not want to wait for the sergeant captains of our missing galleys to arrive before we start spreading false rumours. I want to start spreading them as soon as possible.

"Alright, lads, here's the plan. We'll be leaving here and rendezvousing in Malta as soon as the rest of our galleys arrive and the weather looks good.

"In the meantime, you can give your crews short, two-hour shore leaves during daylight hours. Time to wet their whistles and dip their dingles. But only a few men at a time and no one is to be allowed ashore after dark.

"I want you all to make sure your men understand why they must always stay close to their vessels and their weapons—both because every cog and galley must always be ready to repel boarders in case the Moors come with their galleys and because, depending on the weather, we'll probably be leaving on short notice and heading for Malta. We'll leave on the first good weather as soon as the rest of our galleys come through the harbour entrance and can take on the necessary water and supplies."

Young Peter Sergeant looked confused after I finished speaking to the sergeant captains and sent them back in their dinghies to their galleys and cogs. He'd heard me asking our pilots what they know about Algiers and watched intently during our voyage as I studied the two maps I'd bought off the mapmaker in Lisbon.

Indeed, Peter had been with me when I bought the

maps in Lisbon and sat there quietly whilst I spent an entire afternoon plying the mapmaker and his assistant with questions about Algiers and the pirates based there. He had expected to hear me say we'd be going to Algiers.

I tried to explain things to Peter after the sergeant captains rowed away in their dinghies.

I'm trying to learn him, aren't I?

"Do you understand what I'm trying to do by telling the captain sergeants we'll be heading for Malta from here, Peter? Of course you do; or you will, if you think about it.

"Consider this," I told him quietly so none of the crew around us could hear what I said.

"Many of the people here on the island are Moslems and they and all the merchants undoubtedly have dealings with the Algerians and all the other Moslem pirates, despite the war going on between their various rulers and priests.

"We want the word to get out to the merchants and taverns and churches about our plans to sail to Malta from here—because we're not going to Malta."

Chapter Two
The men learn of my plan.

Our twelfth and final galley rowed into Palma's harbour this morning, and Harold and the pilots agreed the weather looks promising. Accordingly, early in the afternoon, after a final visit to the harbour tavern for a bowl and a chop, I pissed in the harbour and ordered Peter to run up the flag calling my sergeant captains to a meeting.

They'd seen the last of our galleys come in earlier today, and my summons was expected. Within the minute the sergeant captains were all in their dinghies and being rowed to where my galley was moored against the quay. Some of them were wearing their hooded, leather tunics. It was chilly on the water even though it was a beautiful spring day in early April.

My message was short and sweet, and I winked at Peter after I said it.

"All of our galleys are now here and we'll be sailing for Malta in a few hours. So all of you must stop granting shore leaves to your men and immediately send parties ashore to recall your leave men who are already there.

"We'll need all of our men for the trip, so I want all of you whose galleys are at the quay to immediately move them to the harbour and anchor them there so our men can't run or slip ashore for one last drink or dingle dip.

"My galley will stay here at the quay and board those of your men who return from leave after you anchor in the harbour. I'll bring them out to you later. Dismissed."

Three hours later and the flag went up again to call another meeting of the sergeant captains. Most of their shore parties and leave-men had already returned, and all of our galleys were now anchored in the harbour and provisioned and ready to go.

Harold had also moved our galley out into the harbour, and this time the meeting was not short and sweet.

"Everyone, listen up," I said as I raised my hands for silence. "Here is information for your ears only and not to be shared with any member of your crew until we clear the harbour—our galleys are not going from here to Malta and then on to Cyprus. We're going to make a slight detour; as soon as the weather looks good, we are going to take our galleys into Algiers looking for prizes and then go on to Malta with any we take."

There were cheers and smiles all around, and rightly so—almost every man on the deck was on our raid into Tunis and had profited greatly from it; and those who hadn't been to Tunis had certainly heard all about it. Then I continued with the best of all possible good news—this time the prize money would be even greater.

"Prize money will be as follows: sergeant captains will receive three bezant gold coins for every galley or cog or other cargo transport their galley or its prize crews take and get to Malta; sergeants who aren't on a prize crew, three silver coins; and every man twenty copper coins. Every man of every rank will also get another two coppers for each additional vessel his galley and its prize crews burn.

"And that's not all—sergeants who become prize captains will get two gold coins and keep their prize as its sergeant captain if they get it to Malta; their prize sergeants will get nine silvers and their prize crewmen sixty coppers. Fishing boats and fishermen are to be left alone as always."

Yes, we're generous, but we're not dumb; even the meanest galleys and cogs were worth much more than the prize money we'd be paying to get them—and burned galleys can't be used against us.

Loud cheers and even bigger smiles were the order of the day when the captains heard the prize monies they'd receive for the prizes they take and burn. All but two of the sergeant captains were with us on our visit to Tunis last year and what they are now being offered is a chance for advancement for their men—and riches beyond their dreams for themselves.

There was, of course, the not-so-little matter of actually getting to Algiers and actually taking prizes and actually getting them to Malta.

The only men not smiling were our two cog captains—they were not going to accompany us to Algiers. So I took great pains to console them.

And rightly so, as I later explained to Peter Sergeant. Albert from Devon, the captain of one of them, was one of the original archers and deserved to know he was not being slighted. And, for that matter, so does William from Chester who was the archer sergeant captaining the other cog.

"Don't worry, you two—you and your men will get the very same prize money for every pirate galley or Saracen cargo vessel you take from this moment on. So, you and your crews are likely to end up with more prize money than anyone else by the end of the sailing season.

"You can sail from here to anywhere you wish and begin baiting them to attack your cogs as soon as our galleys clear the harbour for Algiers. Send your prizes to Cyprus by whatever route sounds best. You and your men will collect your prize coins on the Limassol quay just like everyone else.

"Oh yes, and each and every one of you must make damn sure your prize sergeants and crews understand they'll need to have enough water in their skins or a good plan as to where they'll get some on their way to Cyprus."

Then we got down to seriously planning our raid and arranging for the cogs to pass out the extra candle lanterns and incendiary bundles of dried twigs they'd been carrying as cargo without even their sergeant captains knowing why.

Two days later, the weather looked good for reaching the harbour at Algiers during the Moors' special prayers which, as everyone knows, start at noon on Friday. Friday being the Islamic Sabbath and the day Moslems are most likely to be in their onion-shaped churches praying to their heathen gods. It's what I've always been told whenever I asked the Moslem merchants we've encountered—and I devoutly hope it's true for it is always best to try to steal something when its owner isn't around to try to stop you.

It was crisp and clear with winds from the north when I ordered Peter Sergeant to raise the "follow me" flag on Wednesday in the early afternoon, and then nodded to Harold. A few shouted orders from Harold and the anchor of his big galley was raised and his rowers were in their places. Everyone was obviously waiting for the signal and ready to go—a few seconds later, the sound of many rowing drums began to boom and a long line of galleys followed us out of the Palma harbour.

The men on our prize-taking cogs were crowding their rails and waving down to us and cheering as we rowed past them. I could see Albert Devon high above me on his cog and we exchanged friendly salutes and waves as our galley passed by on its port side. The cogs were now free to be on their way to troll for pirates whenever their sergeant captains consider the wind and weather to be favourable.

As soon as our galleys cleared the harbour entrance, they moved in and closed up tight around us. We'll stay close together all day and, when the sun finishes passing overhead, we'll use the light from the candle lamps on our masts in an effort to remain close together in tonight's darkness.

Hanging a candle lamp on their masts was important, I'd explained to the sergeant captains, because we want our galleys to stay together so we can go in to the Algiers harbour in one big group Friday morning—to push a heavy English arrow into the heart of the Moorish pirates was how I put it.

According to all the information Harold and I have been able to gather, the Algerians are most likely at prayers when the sun is directly overhead on Fridays. According to Harold and those who are supposed to know about such things, noon on Friday is when the Moorish galleys and cargo transports in the Algiers harbour are most likely to be empty of everyone except their slaves and either moored or pulled up on the beach so they can't float away.

Cutting out their galleys and transports whilst the pirates were praying worked for us at Tunis, and we were all hoping it will work for us again here at Algiers.

Attacking when they're distracted by other things and least expect an attack is always the best policy when fighting Moslems—and everyone else.

****** *William*
The weather was favourable and our brightly lit

candle lanterns enabled us to stay together under the stars of mostly clear skies both Wednesday and Thursday night. The arrival of the sun on Friday morning found us bobbing in the water just off the coast near Algiers with our men fully rested and ready to go. Harold and I looked at each other and we both nodded our heads.

"Hang the 'follow me' flag and the 'attack' flag on the mast," Harold bellowed at the chosen man he'd had standing ready at the mast ever since the sun came up. He and the other galley captains will be using their sails and having their men rowing easy to conserve their strength until we reach the harbour entrance.

I watched with appreciation as our galleys immediately, and very prematurely, formed into the attack formation we'll use when we pass through the harbour entrance. After a while, Peter fetched me my iron helmet and sword and one of the small, round shields hanging on the deck railing. I was already wearing my chain shirt and had my longbow and quivers of arrows slung over my shoulder.

Everyone was ready for a fight, including me— Peter and I are both carrying our longbows and two quivers of iron-tipped arrows. Peter's got a small shield and sword as well and a borrowed helmet which looks like it doesn't fit as well as mine.

The other archers on board Harold's galley were similarly equipped. Whilst we watched, they untied and spread out on the deck all of the many bales of arrows we have on board. Without a doubt, similar preparations were underway on every one of our galleys.

Chapter Three
We visit Algiers

Algiers is a huge city with a superb natural harbour. It's an altogether impressive place with a couple of beautiful, white, sandy beaches and houses with red tile roofs running up from the city's long wood and stone quay to the city walls, and then beyond the walls on the far side of the city—all the way up to the great fortress crowning the hill which towers above the city and its harbour.

More than twenty thousand people are said to live inside Algiers' city walls and as many again outside of them. And, if half the stories I've been told are true, they are all apparently either pirates or merchants or their slaves and servants.

Our tightly grouped galleys split into three separate smaller groups as we come through the harbour entrance with the rowing drum of every galley beating a fast and steady beat and two men at every oar.

Four of our galleys are going for the many Algerian galleys nosed into the beach to the north of the quay; four to the quay itself to take the galleys and cogs moored along it; and four to take those anchored in the harbour.

There are also a few galleys and a lot of fishing boats all along the beach south of the harbour. If all goes well, we may try to get some of those galleys on the way out.

People were standing on the beach and the quay casually watching as we rowed in. We were obviously a curiosity since there were so many galleys coming into the harbour at the same time. They just stood there and watched until the first of our galleys reached the beach and the quay and the men of our prize crews began jumping off them carrying weapons.

Everything changed when the Algerians saw our men jump off their galleys carrying weapons. Some of the watchers began running for the nearby houses and for the gates in the city wall, particularly the gate which seemed to lead up to the big church in the middle of the city; others began running towards the quay and the galleys on the beach. Most, however, just stood there and watched.

****** *Sergeant Captain Edward Heath*
Captain William assigned me to go after the Algerian galleys pulled up side by side on the harbour beach next to the quay. My crew and I are as prepared and determined as men can be. This is the chance of a lifetime for me to become rich and famous. As you might imagine, I am determined not to let it pass.

I've named off the men for three prize crews and

they're all ready and anxious to fight their way on to an Algerian galley and take it off the beach. Then, God willing, they'll sail them on to Malta and Cyprus and I'll be rich.

My new wife is very enthusiastic about this. She's a widow I met on board one of our refugee-carrying galleys when it carried her to safety from Latika. That's where I made my mark and signed on with the archers as a pilot.

As you might imagine, we want to cut our prizes out and get away with them quickly before the heathen bastards begin to fight back. That's why I am standing here in the bow looking for galleys which are merely nosed into the beach next to the quay and still floating—so my prize crews can quickly push them off the beach and climb aboard. If a galley doesn't have slaves to help my prize crew row it to Malta, we'll burn it, if we have time, and look for one with slaves who can do the rowing.

"Over there. Put us in there," I shouted over my shoulder to my rudder man as I pointed to a couple of Algerian galleys nosed into the beach side by side.

"Stand by to back oars—back oars."

There was a grinding noise for a couple of seconds as the bow of our hull began to come over the sand and pebbles at the shoreline and my galley lurched to a stop.

Even before we'd come completely to a stop, there were great cheers and shouts and more than half my archers and sailors, the men of my three prize crews, jumped over the deck railing in front of me to wade ashore and go for the galleys. Every man was a volunteer because of the coins and promotions on offer, and those of my men who weren't selected were jealous of them.

Every man in my prize crews was carrying small shields and swords, and about half of them were also carrying longbows and quivers. Three of them, one member of each my three prize crews, were carrying bundles of twigs and a lantern to fire them if his prize crew comes across a galley it cannot take. And they'll do if they can; there's prize money in burning them too if they have no slaves.

Every copper counts, you know. That's what my wife always says.

Removing the weight of all the men in my prize crews from the front of my galley raised our bow and, as expected, we floated free. One of my chosen men jumped down to follow the prize crews. His name is Joseph and he'd stand there, knee deep in the water, and use the mooring line he's holding to keep our galley close to shore until all of my men were either back on board or safely away in our prizes. Three others of my men were on deck holding long-bladed pikes and ready to push us away from shore for a fast departure as soon as Joseph scrambled back on board.

Already two of my prize crews were climbing on the two side-by-side galleys floating next to us with their noses up on the beach. My third prize crew was dashing down the beach to a third galley about three hundred paces further to the north. The sand might be loose higher up on the beach and slow them down, so they were mostly running along the water's edge where the sand might be firmer and let them run faster. It's something we talked about yesterday.

Resistance. By God, we are meeting resistance.

I could hear the shouts and sounds of fighting coming from inside the two side-by-side Algerian galleys beached next to us. Worse, there were armed men standing on the sand in front of the third galley and more jumping down from it. My prize crew running down the beach was about to be in a serious fight.

"Francis," I snapped to the newly promoted archer sergeant standing next to me as I pointed at the galley down the beach where our men were about to come to grips with the Moslems and start fighting. "Take your men down the beach and join the prize crew fighting for that galley; Jack, you take your men and help clear the two galleys next to us."

Almost immediately, there was fighting and shouting all along the beach. Worse, it appeared my third prize crew and their reinforcements had run into a wasp's nest of Saracens or Algerians or whatever they're called. They were heavily engaged on the beach to my right and more of the heathens were coming. Francis's archers were not going to be enough.

"Everyone, follow me. Emergency. Emergency. Let's go. Hurry, boys, hurry."

I grabbed a small shield off the railing where they hang and rushed down the beach at the head of twenty or so of my men; they were the last of my crew except for the minimal number of rowers we'll need to get off the beach and row away. Already some of my boarding party had been cut down.

Our arrival made the difference. Many of the Algerians began to run away; others were still fighting but the tide of the battle was definitely turning more and more unfavourable. Some of my men were down but most of them were at the galley; they're trying to push it out and climb aboard at the same time.

"Push it out. That's it. Push it out. Everyone get on board. Hurry."

I was shouting encouragements and running for the galley myself when, suddenly, a tremendous blow to my back caused me to lose a step and stagger forward. I looked down when I was able to regain control of my feet without actually falling. A bloody arrowhead was sticking out of my chest in front of me. Then somehow I was on the beach and I could see legs around me and sand was getting into my eyes.

I'm killed. Poor old Jane. She's a widow ag—

****** *William*

Harold headed our galley for the Algerian transports and galleys tied up along the long, stone quay. Our designated place among our four galleys heading for the quay was in the middle left of whatever shipping is tied up along it.

One of our galleys was coming up behind us very fast, too fast I thought, and already pulling alongside of us. It was going after the galleys and cogs moored further to our left on the quay. The other two are going to those moored to our right.

A few minutes earlier Harold had told everyone to piss on the deck and now the rowing drum was beating at an unsustainable rate. I could feel my heart pounding and was glad I pissed when everyone else did.

I don't know why but it seems a lot of men always need to piss before a battle. I know I always do. It seems strange, but there you are.

As we approached the quay, Harold shouted, "Rowers, stop." And then after a very brief pause, he shouted what the rowers expected to hear next.

"Back oars. Pull back. Pull back. Pull. Pull. Prize crews and deck archers. Get ready. Prize men and deck archers. Get ready."

There was a hard bump and the sound of splintering wood as we banged hard into the quay between two moored Algerian galleys. We hit so hard the upper part of the deck railing in our bow splintered and some of the men standing ready to leap on to the quay lost their balance.

The men quickly recovered and within seconds, Harold's prize crews began pouring off the deck. Some of the archers were carrying four or five quivers of arrows and a sword and small shield as well. It seemed a mere blink of the eye before they were pounding down the quay and racing each other to be the first to reach the potential prizes moored along it.

Me? I was standing next to the railing around the roof of the forward castle and gripping the railing tightly, although I didn't realise it at the time. It was exciting.

It was almost as if I was under some kind of spell. I seemed to be seeing everything very clearly, and I was surprised because it seemed as though everything had somehow slowed down and was moving very slowly, even the rapidly running men. I had my bow strung and an arrow notched, but there was no enemy to push an arrow towards. Harold was standing next to me shouting orders. I can't remember a thing he said.

Harold and I remained on the castle roof with a wide-eyed Peter standing next to me with his longbow strung and one of his heavy arrows notched and ready to push. Like me, he too saw no targets. Harold was standing next to me holding his big shield and his sword drawn. There were four of Harold's best archers on the roof with us.

We watched as one of our boarding parties ran to the Algerian galley on our left and the other ran to the big cargo cog on our right. The men were running hard and didn't have far to go. They reached their potential prizes and rushed aboard them in what now seems like the blink of an eye but at the time seemed to take forever.

Those of our galley's archers not assigned to a prize crew were on the roof of the castle with us. They initially pushed a few arrows at the handful of unarmed Algerians standing on the quay even before our boarding parties pour off our deck and on to the quay.

"Don't waste your arrows," I remember snapping at them. "You'll need them soon enough." *My prediction came true all too soon.*

Peter and I just stood there and stared and listened. There may have been no armed resistance but there certainly was much shouting and commotion both on the quay and on the Algerian galleys on either side of us. Harold just stood there next to us with one of the big shields we use when we fight on land. He's obviously poised to throw it up for us to hide behind if arrows start coming the other way.

All of a sudden, Harold dropped his shield and motioned for me to stay put. He jumped down on to the deck and then vaulted over the deck railing and on to the quay to better watch the progress of our boarding parties. After a brief look, he vaulted back over rail and was back on board with a big smile and a pleasing report. All three of his boarding parties are on their intended prizes and their mooring lines have been cut or cast off. It was time to move out into the harbour and search for another prize.

"Archers below to row. Steer to the big one over there," Harold shouts to the rudder man as the rowing drum begins to beat. "Yes. The big one, the one with three masts and the square sails. Go for it. Hurry, damn you. Hurry. She's raising her anchor."

And then a few minutes later. . . .

"Grapplers, archers, and number three boarding party men to the deck. Grapplers, archers, and number three boarding party to the deck. Get ready, lads. Here come more coins for us all. Throw your grapples as she comes. Throw. Throw. Stand by with the tow line."

The ship Harold was after is one of the biggest ships I've ever seen. It had three tall masts, square sails, and a strange black flag with Islamic markings in white. *Wonder where it's from? Well, I guess we're about to find out.*

"What kind of ship is that, Harold? I've never seen one like that before."

"First time for me, too. Big'un, isn't she, by God? Eighty paces long if she's a foot, and three masts. I think she's one of those new heathen ships I heard about after the goddamn Moors catched me up as a slave.

"I saw a ship sort of like it through my oar hole once when I was rowing for the Moors, didn't I? In Acre, it was . . . when the Saracens held the castle and the Moors was still welcome. Square sails, it had, and three masts . . . not as big as this one though."

We watched and nodded with satisfaction as Harold's sailors threw their grappling irons and began hauling on their lines to pull our galley up against it. About then was when Harold and I suddenly realised the problem at the same moment. The ship we wanted to take as a prize and had successfully grappled was big, very big—there was no way a prize crew could climb up on to its deck and seize it because its deck was so high above the deck of our galley.

One part of the big ship's deck looked to be lower, so Harold ordered some of the grapplers to loosen their lines so the others could pull us forward along its hull to reach the low spot. It took time but our sailors managed to pull us forward to the low spot on the ship's deck—and then we discovered the big three-masted ship still towered too far above us even at its lowest point.

This was impossible.

"Cut the lines," Harold shouted with an exasperated sound in his voice. "We'll go for another."

****** *William*

The lines were cut, and we started to go for a nearby cog. But as we got closer, we could see its deck crowded with armed men. And then rocks start coming down around us.

They've got slingers, by God.

"Don't throw," Harold screams at the sailors who are winding up to throw with the grapples they are swinging around and around over their heads. "Don't throw, damn it. Row to the small one over there instead. Yes, that's the one."

One of our sailors on the deck below me suddenly dropped, as if he'd been axed, as we went under the bow of the second cog and moved towards the third. Then another staggered and sat down on the deck with an arrow in his thigh.

Damn. Those bastards up there are good. I wonder why they're not at the Moorish church in the city? Could it be they're not Moors?

I jumped down and ran to the mast and climbed part way up it for a look as we rowed our way towards our latest intended prize. Overall, we were doing quite well. One of our galleys was coming towards us with a cog in tow. Other galleys, clearly prizes, were rowing for the harbour entrance along with some of our own galleys. And then I saw it—one of our galleys seemed to be stuck broadside to the beach next to the quay with fighting going on all around it.

"Harold, over there," I shouted as I pointed at the fighting going on around the galley, which had somehow gotten itself turned sideways to the beach. Then I ran back to the castle roof after I burned my hands sliding down the rope ladder too fast.

"Edward Heath's galley is still on the beach. It looks stuck. Row over there and we'll try to pull him off. Quickly, man, quickly."

A few minutes of hard rowing was all it took before we approached Edward's stricken galley. Its stern had floated around so it was floating broadside up against the beach—and there was a great horde of Algerian men on the beach around it and more in the shallow water trying to climb on board. Even worse, a great mob of men was running towards it from all over the beach and from the city walls.

Oh my God.

The oars of Edward's besieged galley were not moving. Every man on it was probably on its deck fighting the enemy boarders who were continuing to climb on board. And even if there were rowers still on the benches, they wouldn't be able to get their shore-side oars into the water to get it moving. We could hear the shouts and screams and the sound of the hand-to-hand fighting coming to us over the water.

As we approached Edward's stricken galley, our archers began pushing arrow after arrow at the Algerians they could see on its deck and those on the beach coming to climb aboard. So did Peter and I. We reaped a deadly harvest and it was a chaotic scene on the deck of Edward's galley and on the beach with much shouting and screaming. Everything was happening at once.

Two of Harold's sailors were in the very front of our galley getting ready to throw the grapples they were swinging around their heads. Our quickly agreed plan was simple and the only one with any chance of success—clear the deck of Algerians with our longbows whilst our sailors hook on to Edward's galley with their grapples and pull it away from the shore.

It was instantly apparent to everyone that merely helping Edward's men clear the Algerians off their deck would not be enough to save them; we also had to stop the horde of Algerians rushing towards it from getting on board to join the fighting.

Then more disaster. One of the swinging grapple irons hit a nearby archer in the head and down he went with the arrow he was about to launch skittering off into the sky. The other grapple, thank God, landed and hooked on to the railing of Edward's embattled galley on its right rear, near the stern.

"Back oars. Every man except the archers on the castle roofs to the oars. Every man except the archers on the castle roofs to the oars. Pull. Pull. Pull."

Our oars literally beat the water to a froth as our drummer beat the rowing drum harder and harder amidst the rowing sergeant's cries to dig deep and pull hard—and for a while nothing happened. Finally, the stern of our stranded galley began to slowly come off the beach and swing around towards us.

It was coming slowly, too slowly. The fighting and what was left of Edward's crew became even more visible once Edward's galley began to come off the beach, so we were even closer to where they were standing and fighting. Edward was not among them.

We pushed our arrows at the Algerians whenever we could get a clear shot but mostly we watched helplessly as the rapidly dwindling survivors of Edward's crew gave ground and were pushed backwards towards where our grapple was attached.

Someone still standing among our men on board was obviously smart enough to realise their only hope of escape was to prevent the grappling line from being cut. He was right. If we could pull Edward's galley out deep enough into the water no more of the Algerians on the beach would be able to climb on board to join the fight.

Too late. We were starting to pull Edward's galley stern first away from the shore when the sound of the fighting on its deck slowly died away. Suddenly, the grapple line went slack and there was great cheering and shouting on the galley's deck despite our continuing storm of arrows—and it wasn't in English.

Poor Edward.

****** *William*

Amidst the turmoil and confusion whilst we were trying to retrieve Edward's galley, I could see some of our other galleys and more of what are obviously prizes rowing and sailing for the harbour entrance and bound for

Malta.

Others of our galleys and prizes have already passed through the entrance and are disappearing into the distance. I could also see smoke coming from one of the Algerian galleys anchored in the harbour and from a couple of galleys at the far end of the beach. They must not have had slaves to row them away.

There was activity all along the beach and in the harbour. It was like a wasp's nest that has been overturned. Small boats were everywhere coming and going from the cogs in the harbour. Worse, there was a great deal of activity on the galleys and cogs we didn't take or burn. Their crews were on their decks to repel boarders—too late, of course, since we were leaving.

But some of them are obviously preparing to get underway to escape—or to counter-attack and try to retake our prizes? Look there; that one's oars are starting to move. And there's another.

It's time to go.

"Make for the harbour entrance," I ordered Harold.

"We'll block it as long as possible and then do a wounded bird."

We must block it. Some of our galleys and prizes may not have a full complement of rowers and be caught by the fast movers coming out of the wasp's nest we kicked over.

Chapter Four
We are pursued.

We reached the harbour entrance and waited as the last two of our galleys and a couple of prizes rushed past. We could hear the fast pace of their rowing drums as they moved past us. In a few minutes, they would be over the horizon towards the south and out of sight to any pursuers.

Spirits were high and the handful of men on our decks gave each other cheers and waves as the galley and their prizes go past. It's little wonder the galley decks were so empty; almost everyone was at an oar helping to row their galley out of the harbour at the highest possible speed. That's exactly where they should be.

"All archers on deck," Harold shouted, even though most of them were already there. *Poor Harold; I think he's a bit embarrassed by taking so few prizes compared to the other captains.*

The cheers on the decks were barely gone when Harold turned us towards the north and we began very slowly rowing away using only the oars on our lower benches—like the bird who pretends to be wounded to lure the fox away from the nest.

It was the ruse we planned to use to gull any pursuers and it's why we sailed with so many men including a good number of the company's strongest rowers. And, of course, damn it, one of our prize crews was still on board to help with the rowing needed to keep us ahead of any pursuers.

A full ten minutes passed before the first of the Algerian galleys came charging out of the harbour. We were the closest raider in sight and it headed straight for us with the water from its oars flashing in the sunlight. They were pulling hard.

The Algerian began to close the gap on us as two more Algerian galleys came out of the harbour, one after another, right behind it. Our other galleys and prizes were pulling away from us in the distance with the last of them just going over the horizon.

We are by far the closest enemy galley and trying to look slow and vulnerable with our square sail only half up and flapping as if some of its lines have been cut.

It seemed to be working. All three of the Algerians headed our way as the harbour entrance began to recede from view. Hopefully, any subsequent galleys coming out will follow the three chasing us northward.

Our drum began to pick up the beat as the first of our pursuers closed on us. The other two Algerians, and possibly two more according to the lookout on our mast, were coming after us as well. Harold himself scampered up the mast for a look.

"It's nowhere near time yet," he shouted at me breathlessly as he climbed back down. "There are four of them behind yon thruster and they are still coming."

An hour passed and then another started. Our flight continued and our pursuers stayed with us. The wind was from the west when Harold came down from another look from the mast and slowly reduced the rowing beat.

Almost an hour or so earlier, one of the last of the pursuing galleys out of the harbour was able catch up and pass our initial pursuer. It was now the only Algerian in sight and it followed us and cut the corner to close rapidly when Harold made a dogleg turn to the right.

Hopefully, we and our pursuer are far enough ahead of the other Algerian galleys so they didn't see either of us make the turn. We certainly didn't want them to make it—fighting one galley at a time is best.

"Peter, go up on mast to the lookout's nest and keep watch. No. Don't take your bow or quiver. Leave them here on the deck with me. You'll need both hands to hold on to the rope."

Twenty minutes later and it appeared the trailing Algerians were so far back they missed our turn and are no longer following us. Now we're heading straight into the wind and it's just between us and our one remaining pursuer.

Well, it's just between the two of us if Harold's right about the other Algerians not making the turn to continue following us. In any event, our pursuer was finally closing on us.

I trusted Harold and the sailor he has as a lookout on the mast. But I wasn't taking any chances— every so often I sent Peter up to the lookout's nest to make sure no other Algerians were in sight.

Harold had all of our archers on deck and on the castle roofs and in the lookout's nest as our pursuer continued to cut the gap separating us. He let the Algerian close on us until it was well within the range of our archers because of the favourable winds.

That's when our archers began to launch and the drum picked up the beat so we'd stay just enough ahead to keep the Algerian within range of our archers' longbows.

I myself climbed up the mast almost to the lookout's nest to watch as the archers in the nest above me and those on the castle roofs below me began to push out their arrows.

Climbing a galley's mast almost to its lookout nest is not an easy thing to do. I'd done it a few times before and it wasn't something I enjoyed. The damn rope ladder always seems to be slippery and it sways back and forth, don't you know.

I stopped climbing when I was just below the archers in the lookout's nest and holding on to the swaying rope ladder for dear life. In the distance I could see movement on the Algerian's deck as our archers' arrows found the range and began to land. Now the tables were turning.

At first, the Algerian thruster merely slowed

slightly to drop back out of range. We, of course, promptly slowed with it so it couldn't escape the continuous rain of our arrows.

Finally, the Algerians had enough and turned to break off—and we turned back to go after them.

Harold quickly spun our galley around using both its rudder and oars and then we rowed hard to get a little behind and slightly off to the port side of our now fleeing prey. From this angle, the arrows of our archers can drop into the open area behind the Algerian's mast and reach down to its rudder men and some of its rowers—and some of them do.

It didn't take very long. Within minutes the Algerian was virtually dead in the water with its deck and upper rowing bank clear of men. At some point the Algerian captain finally realised our need for a specific position in order to drop arrows into the open area next to his lower rowing benches. He had his rowers periodically row on only one side so that his galley kept turning in a tight circle to keep us from having clear shots.

It was almost a game. The Algerian captain was constantly turning to deny our archers a shooting line into his rudder men and the open area on his lower deck where his survivors were hiding—and we were constantly moving around his galley to get clear shots into it for our archers, particularly those on the castle roofs and in the lookout's nest.

Harold finally brought us alongside the Algerian about an hour before the sun finished passing overhead. I was down from the mast by then and our archers were all on deck with their short-distance, heavy arrows. The archers on the castle roofs and in the lookout's nest had already cleared the Algerian's deck and its upper rowing benches on one side.

There were no Algerians in sight as our grappling irons were thrown. With the sun about to finish passing overhead, it was now or never.

The shuddering crash as our two hulls came together brought the surviving Algerians out from behind the nearside deck railing, where they'd been sheltering, and charging out of the lower rowing deck—and straight into an absolute storm of arrows from the archers lining the side of our galley.

In an instant, Peter and I and every archer were shooting arrows at close range as some of the Algerians launched their forlorn hope and went down, many with multiple arrows in them. The few survivors quickly dropped back down to cower and try to stay out of sight.

For a while, the two galleys bobbed up and down together and there was no movement on the Algerian. All we could see were bodies on the Algerian's deck and neither galley dared send a man up its mast to look at the other for fear he'd be picked off by an archer.

Finally, there was a loud hail in a strange foreign tongue and then in bad French. "Quarter. Quarter. We surrender."

****** *William*
It was totally dark, and the warm and sunny day

had turned into a chilly and windy evening by the time we cast off the grappling lines and our prize crew and the Algerian's released slaves began rowing Harold's fourth prize towards Malta.

All of the Algerian sailors except the most seriously wounded had been chained to the lower rowing benches and food and water from our stores quickly loaded; the Algerian's joyful and newly freed slaves were enthusiastically helping to row and wolfing down food.

The big difference as the Algerian galley got underway for Malta was the surviving Algerians had taken the place of their slaves as the principal rowers— and their newly released slaves were wolfing down the bread and cheese and drinking the water we'd hurriedly passed over to our prize crew whilst it was still light enough to see what we were doing.

We'd ended the day with one man killed and three wounded, one so seriously with a cracked skull he might need a mercy. Blood must have seeped into the water for we soon attract a large number of sharks. They were undoubtedly feasting on the Algerian bodies we threw overboard.

The surviving Algerians were brave men who tried to recover from our surprise attack and fight us. We've got them chained, of course, but we'll feed them, treat them well, and try to exchange them, even their wounded.

Hell, we're the pirates; they were our prey even though they didn't know it until it was too late for them to escape.

Chapter Five

Gathering our prizes.

Our arrival in Malta five days later was quite triumphant. About half of our galleys and prizes were already here when we came in. Their crews lined their decks to cheer and wave as we rowed into the harbour at Valletta and tied up at the city's old stone quay. The day may have been a bit murky and overcast, but everyone's spirits were sky high and rightly so.

Even Count Brindisi, Malta's somewhat Catholic ruler on behalf of the King of Sicily, came down from the stone watch tower on the hill that passes for his castle and was standing at the quay to greet us as we tied up. At Brindisi's insistence, he and I promptly walked to the nearest tavern so he could hear all about the raid and, of course, get the latest news about King Richard and the latest gossip about our betters. I think he really believed it when he claimed his fortune teller had predicted our success and Richard's return.

Brindisi obviously admires King Richard. How surprising. Are Thomas and I the only ones who despise him because he broke his word and murdered the thousands of Saracens who surrendered to us at Acre?

It came to me as we were sitting there laughing and drinking and telling stories that the old scoundrel was jealous; I think he misses his days as a pirate before he got made a noble for using his galleys to help the current King of Sicily take its throne when the old king died childless.

I'm sure he is—living in a cold and drafty stone tower in your very own castle sounds wonderful until you have one and have to live in it. A nice comfy farmhouse with cattle and sheep packed into the lower room to keep it warm is much more comfortable.

****** *William*

Seven happy, drunken days later, the weather began to clear and we prepared to row out of Malta and on to Cyprus with big hangovers. Alfred Forester's galley will wait for a while to gather up any late arrivals.

On the bad side, the butcher's bill was high even before we know the fate of the fifty or so men in our two missing prize crews. We have almost certainly lost at least one of our galleys and at least ninety-seven men including two of our sergeant captains, mostly from our lost galley. We have forty-seven wounded ranging from dying and seriously wounded men who will stay on Malta under the care of the local barber to those who were only slightly sliced and have already returned to duty.

On the good side, we've taken three cogs including one with a cargo of fine olive oil and eighteen Algerian galleys have already come in with our prize crews in command. There are still two prizes missing and, as expected, there has been no word from our two pirate-taking cogs. They should be cruising between here and the Malta by now and attracting pirates—who, hopefully, won't discover the number of fighting men on their intended victim until they've lashed themselves to its side and it is too late to escape.

Also on the good side, we are off to Cyprus carrying a diverse cargo—a goodly bag of coins from selling the cargo of olive oil we found in one of the cogs, a couple of Maltese merchants and their goods, two foul smelling Hospitallers, and a party of German knights going out to join the crusade along with their men and their priest.

The lord, or whatever he is, leading the German crusaders was quite upset yesterday when he came to see me in the tavern and I told him what he would have to pay and his men would be split up among our galleys and disarmed to insure my men's safety. But I told him it was take it or leave it, and he took it.

At least, I think the knight was upset. Maybe getting red in the face and shouting is how Germans talk all the time. Probably not; his translator priest seemed rather serene.

Even so, the German will be a worry so long as he is on board because he's either a total blockhead or a religious fanatic with a death wish. Why else would he be leading his men into meaningless battles now that King Guy de Lausignon's stupidity at Hattin destroyed any chance of a crusader victory?

But I couldn't complain about the new King of Cyprus being a moron, could I? He sold me a lordly title for a bag of coins and his crooked chancellor helped Thomas buy his bishopric. Besides, Guy's disastrous defeat at Hattin was what caused all the Christian and Jewish refugees who are making us rich by carrying them to safety in our galleys.

What was absolutely astonishing to my brother Thomas and me was Guy's defeat and capture at Hattin, which quite rightly ended his kingship of Jerusalem, resulted in him becoming the new King of Cyprus. The Christian kings and nobles who ransomed him from the Saracens after Hattin and then helped him buy the Cyprus throne from the Templars for one hundred thousand bezant gold coins were as dumb as stones according to my brother.

Thomas thinks their stupidity and moronic behaviour comes from drinking bad wine, and bodes well for my son's future. I hope he's right.

Thomas is quite knowledgeable about such things and well educated as everyone knows. He speaks Latin and read all nine books at the monastery before my mum died and he left to rescue me and take me crusading with

Richard.

On balance, our success and the prospect of prize money attracted many more recruits in Malta than the few we lost in desertions. Mostly they are young Maltese lads willing to train as archers; although, we did pick up a few sailors and a couple of Brindisi's bored veterans.

It's hard to understand why any of our men would run here on Malta—it's a small island, the wine is too sweet, and tavern girls smell bad. Besides, the men on our successful raid won't receive their prize money until they get their prizes to Cyprus.

******

Whilst we were waiting for the rest of our prizes to arrive, I had time to meet with the local bishop and offer him a reward for any likely young boys he could find who are capable of being learnt to scribe and sum along with George and his chums. I told him they'd be learnt Latin and become priests themselves one day.

And so they will—but not to serve the Church and that's for certain.

The bishop was enthusiastic. He said he'd do it "for the Church" even though I'm sure he thinks we intend to use the boys for fucking the way the priests do now that the Pope has ordered them not to marry. I think he'll do it, and there will be boys waiting when we call in Malta on our way back to England after the sailing season—because I promised to pay him a bezant gold coin for each very smart lad I could take to England to be learnt.

"No, Excellency," I told him for the second or third time as I banged my hand on the wooden table so hard my bowl of wine jumped.

I'm getting aggravated.

"We do not want good-looking, young boys; we only want smart boys who can be learnt to do sums and read and scribe and gobble Latin; we want those who can be smart priests, not religious priests. They can be ugly as sin if they are smart lads and quick to learn."

****** *William*

Our big intake on Malta was from the hundreds of slaves we freed from the Algerian galleys. Most of them quickly made their marks to help us row our prizes in exchange for food and transport to Cyprus and then back to England; the rest took off running as soon as their feet hit dry land.

We've got the slaves who stayed with us on double rations to strengthen them up, and we'll sort them out when we get to Cyprus. If the past is any guide, there will be some men from Britain and a number of potential archers and good sailor men among those who have nowhere to go.

An army of men with no homes to go home to is what they mostly are—and so are we, Thomas and me, except that we have George and each other and three castles including the big one at Restormel with three rooms above its great hall.

It's a good thing we signed up so many of the slaves even though many of them are sick and will die of the coughing pox. Our problem is a happy one—we took so many prizes our galleys will be going out of Malta shorthanded even with the addition of the slaves. Our shortage of fighting men was so great Harold convinced me to change my mind about assigning a hundred archers to one of the prize cogs so it could sail as a pirate-taker. Instead, it and the other two will sail as cargo cogs with only sailors in their crews.

On the other hand, we've got enough sailors because so many of the Algerian slaves were sailors from the cogs and cargo ships taken by the Algerian galleys; it's archers we're short of, particularly those who know how to use a longbow. We don't have any to spare for another pirate-taker.

****** *William*

It was a stirring sight to see and hear as the drums begin to beat and our three new cogs and all but one of our twenty-nine galleys moved out of Valletta's harbour on the last Saturday in April. One of the galleys under Henry from Lewes is staying behind to gather up any late arriving prizes.

I'm not hopeful. Perhaps the last two prizes have been retaken.

We've got candles in the lamps on our masts and once again we'll try to stay together for as long as possible. It's probably not all that important we stay together because it's a rare pirate who is willing go after a war galley. They are, after all, much more likely to be carrying fighting men than valuable cargos.

On the other hand, it's better to be safe than sorry since the Algerians are undoubtedly seriously pissed and may be out in force as a result of our raid—and recognise our prizes as their own and try to take them back. As we well know, even the best crew of sailors and archers can be overwhelmed if they have to fight a large number of enemy galleys or boarders at the same time.

In any event, we stayed together for three days before a passing squall caused us to move apart in the night. In the morning, several of our galleys were visible in the distance but we made no effort to rejoin them.

The days that followed were sunny and the wind favourable, so we only had to row periodically. The men spent their time working on their weapons and clothes and yarning about how they're going to spend their prize money.

****** *William*

Harold and I had spent much of our time after we returned to Malta talking with some of the slaves recently freed by our galleys, particularly those who claimed to be master mariners and tell us they know these seas and the streams along the coasts where water and safety are available. There were likely some strong arms among the Algerian slaves we freed but not an experienced archer among them. We'll have to train those we decide to keep.

Several of the men Harold and I talked with were the masters and sergeants of cargo cogs and other boats before the Moors took them, and claim to be able to read and cipher as well. But it soon became apparent only one them actually possessed both skills. His name was Richard and he was from a village in Kent. He made his mark on the company roll as Richard Kent.

Richard's family, so far as he knows, were serfs or tenant farmers. He wasn't sure. He'd been learnt his sums and letters in the monastery his village priest sold him to as a young boy when the pox took his family in the days when old Henry was king. At least, that's what the monks told him before he ran away from being a novice priest and went to sea from the nearby port of Whitby.

"It's better to be a galley slave," was Richard's only comment when I ask him how he liked being in the monastery. But he can scribe and do sums and was willing to make his mark and join us as a sailor sergeant. I'm going to keep him close to me for a while to see if he might be useful. Anyone who can scribe and sum and distrusts priests can't be entirely hopeless.

Talking with Richard Kent raised an idea I'm going to discuss with Thomas when I get back to England—if the archers and sailors are too set in their ways to learn to read and write, maybe Thomas can find the men we need at the monasteries and we can learn them to be archers and sailors. If not, we'll have to keep looking for boys Thomas can learn to be both and wait for them to grow up.

Chapter Six

A new way to fetch coins.

Cyprus was joyful and pleasing as we rowed into the Limassol harbour on a wonderful, early summer day. It was like coming home and, truth be told, in many ways it has become my home.

It's certainly a nicer place to live than England, at least in the winter, because of the weather. The problem, of course, is what my brother Thomas keeps reminding me—my son and I are English and will always be outsiders here no matter how much we might try to fit in. Also, and much more important, living here would be boring and my brother and I have bigger things in mind for George. Besides, the summers in Cyprus are too damn hot.

****** *William*

Yoram and a number of our men were waiting at the quay as I vaulted over the galley's deck rail to join them. Yoram got a big embrace and there were big smiles and handshakes and back slapping all around. I was glad to be here and there's no denying it.

Of course, Yoram got a big embrace and I hugged him off the ground and danced him around. We're friends who have been through a lot together—and I wanted to establish his importance in the eyes of our new men. There are a lot of eyes on us and the word will get around.

And, by God, there's Brian and Henry!

"Brian, is that you? Can it be?" And another big hug, although, this time I'm a lot more careful and don't pick him up and swing him about. Brian's got a bad leg, doesn't he? And good old Henry gets a big handshake and a hearty clap on both shoulders for the good man he is.

We four walked arm in arm up the beach with a big and happy crowd following behind and everyone talking and waving their arms about. Good friends, being alive and unhurt after a battle, and prize money will do that for you every time. My young helpers and fetchers, Peter Sergeant and Richard Kent, followed behind us and took it all in.

****** *William*

Yoram quickly brought me up to date and his report was quite interesting. The six galleys we sent back from England last fall have been bringing in a constant stream of refugees and lots of coins—lots and lots of coins and refugees.

Many of the coins they bring are coming from the payments we receive for carrying refugees and pilgrims.

But others are coins being sent by merchants and others who are willing to pay us to hold their coins safe until they can show up with the proper parchments and claim them.

They are depositing coins with us for safekeeping?

"When did this depositing thing start, Yoram? Who is doing it?"

"At first it was the leather merchants from a village outside Acre. They buy their leather from Cyprus and don't want to chance losing their payment coins to pirates as they have in the past. So they offered to pay us a fee if we would carry their coins here and guard them until they need to spend them. I, of course, accepted—can't go wrong by taking coins, can I?

"Then the story of what the leather men were doing got around and others began sending us their coins to get them safely out of the Holy Land in case the Saracens come and they have to run for it.

"It's turning into a good way to fetch coins. It all started when we charged a fee to carry coins here for one of the leather merchants so he could buy hides and other things here in Cyprus without having to risk a sea trip.

"And, of course, I'm very careful—I keep all of our coins on one side of my room and all those that belong to others on the other side."

Yoram is seriously worried an effort will be made to seize the coins. He took me up the stair to show them to me—and what I saw surprised me, it truly did. He had so many chests of coins stacked up on both sides of his room there was hardly any space left in the middle for his family.

As soon as I saw the coin chests I knew an attack to rob us wasn't my only concern. I know how heavy a chest of coins is and I was instantly afraid the floor would give way and drop the chests on the archer sergeants sleeping in the room below.

"And all the new galleys will bring in even more coins," Yoram said to me, "a whole lot more."

Well, I certainly understand why Yoram is keeping so many of our archers here as guards.

"Well, I certainly understand why you're keeping so many of our archers here," I told him. "It was a very good decision to hold them here and you were absolutely right to make it."

Another of Yoram's problems was the refugees who came to Cyprus with the coins. He was continuing to employ all the refugees who will work for food—they were already working on a third wall and starting a fourth. And we've got four eighty-oar galleys in various stages of construction and repair in the little boatyard we set up next to the beach last year. The first of them is about ready to launch.

The place was like a beehive and the hive is getting stronger and stronger.

****** *William*

Later that afternoon, as soon as we had a chance to walk together and talk privately, I asked Yoram what else he thought we should be doing.

"There are three things I think we should try to do in order to earn more coins," Yoram suggests very deferentially.

I can tell; he's obviously thought about this for some time. I nodded my agreement to have him tell me what he thinks we should do.

"One is to buy one of the old copper quarries from the Roman days and send some of the people we're feeding there to mine the stones we need for the faces of our new log walls. There's an old quarry fairly close that might be good for us. It's obviously been closed for years, but we can put some of the refugees to reopening it for us and move them there to live and cut stones to face the logs in our new walls.

"Another thing is to buy some of the trees on the King's lands and use some of the refugees to cut them and bring the logs here for use in building our new curtain walls and maybe even use it in our boatyard— except I'm not so sure about using the local wood for building and repairing galleys.

"The local boatwrights don't like the local wood. They say it's too hard to work. They say we can still get good boat-building wood from the Lebanon despite the fighting, even from the Saracen ports, if you can imagine. And it's already cut, isn't it?"

"I thought we were getting the logs we need for the new walls from the local merchants?"

We don't want to alienate the local merchants.

"Well, we are, William, we are; we're buying the logs we're using for the walls from the two local wood merchants. Unfortunately, they don't have any tall trees left to cut.

"They say the problem is the good logs which are tall enough to use in our walls are hard to find. It seems that most of the tall trees still standing on Cyprus are on the King's hunting lands and can't be cut down for us to use."

"All right—we need to get our hands on the quarries and the big trees on the King's land. What's the third thing we should do?"

"It's the big one. I think we should use the additional galleys to expand to serve more cities than just those related to refugees escaping from the Holy Land. Rome and Constantinople would seem to be good places to earn more coins. We've got refugees here who would have paid more if we had offered to take them beyond Cyprus. Then we'd have more coins and fewer refugees to look after."

"Well, you're right about that too—adding more cities to those we already serve is something Thomas and I have been talking about. Malta, for example, comes to mind because it's a good stopping place between England and the Holy Land."

Yoram's a smart fellow, indeed; Thomas is right—he's our most valuable man. Do you suppose it's because he knows how to read and do sums?

Yoram then shyly told me whilst I was gone he took it upon himself to make a couple of changes. One is that he is giving our galley crews much longer shore time so that he always has the archers of at least two galleys, several hundred of them, living in the tented barracks areas inside our defensive walls at all times.

Hmm. Yoram's right; we need some of the archers and a competent fighting captain here all the time, even if it means some of our galleys and sailors have to stand idle in the harbour.

Our coins are supposed to be a secret, so our archers are only told they are on shore to practise their archery and learn to use the newfangled bladed pikes Brian is producing. They practise every day whilst they are on shore. Henry supervises the sergeants conducting the training; Brian supervises the fletchers and smiths making their weapons.

Once the archers are fully learnt up with using pikes, those that have been ashore the longest go back to sea in whichever galley's archers and sailors are in line to take their place.

Yoram's other change has been to start sending our galleys to more ports along the Holy Land coast because "they have rich refugees and merchants too."

Thomas is right. Yoram is our very best man.

****** *William*
On the first evening after my arrival, the six of us who are the company's most senior men got together to sit outside and talk and eat chicken and get ourselves properly tipsy drinking bowls of sweet local wine.

Brian, Henry, Harold, Yoram, and I were sitting on stools outside by the door to our little keep—and Yoram's very pregnant and cheerful Lena was constantly tripping off to bring us bowls of wine and chicken from the kitchen. It was a relaxing time, and we had much to discuss. Thomas Cook came and sat with us when he wasn't running off to sergeant the cooking.

One of the first things I inquired about is the French knight who is the King's cousin and Limassol's governor. Yoram and Henry immediately begin laughing. It seems ever since Thomas told him the assassins would try to kill him he has locked himself in his castle and won't come out unless he is summoned by the King—and going to see the King apparently fears him even more.

After a while, Thomas Cook came and joined us. Thomas is one of our original archers and prefers to stay in camp and supervise the cooking. And a good cook he is.

Thomas is like Henry Lewes—last year he'd decided to stay in Cyprus instead of returning to England with us; he says just the thought of getting seasick again is enough to make him ill.

We talked about everything. Yoram and Henry and Thomas told us what has happened here and in the Holy Land since we left, who's run or died or gotten poxed; Harold and I told them about Tunis and Algiers and the battles we'd fought in England and why. And most of all we talked about what to do with all of our newly arrived cogs and galleys.

My God, we've now got thirty-one galleys and five cogs here and more than two thousand men if you include all the slaves we've freed.

The death of Edmund's wife and children absolutely enraged all the original archers who'd known Edmund, and they growled their approval when I told them how we avenged them. And, of course, both Henry and Brian sat up and listened carefully when they heard our stories about the effectiveness of our bladed pikes and longbows and how we used them.

I told them we needed many more pikes and longbows produced and every archer trained to use them both. They nodded with both determination and the satisfaction which comes from being needed when I told them it was now their highest priority.

My young helpers and fetchers, Peter Sergeant and Richard Kent, sat quietly nearby and listened carefully. They didn't say a word.

We all agreed. There is no question about it—a large force of archers needs to be here on Cyprus as guards at all times because of all the coins that are upstairs in Yoram's room, and because we're such a threat to the pirates and the local governor that they may try to eliminate us.

We also agreed on the need to keep our archers trained up so they don't get themselves deaded because they haven't learnt to use modern weapons or don't have them. *Or, if Thomas is right, they die of a pox because they aren't careful about where they piss and shite and stick their dingles.*

Keeping enough men here and training and equipping them with modern weapons is important. On the other hand, we also need to keep our galleys and cogs constantly at sea with enough archers and sailors so they can earn coins by gathering up refugees and pilgrims and carrying coins and coin-earning parchments and such.

Before we staggered off to sleep, we had an answer everyone seemed to like—we'll establish and equip more companies of archers than we need for our galleys and cogs. Then each time a galley or cog comes in, its sergeant captain and sailors can take it right back out with a fresh company of archers—and leave its current company for training and to act as guards until the company's turn comes to go to sea again.

Up until now, each galley and cog has had its own archers and sailors, we've only recruited when we need to replace men who've been lost or run. But deciding how many additional archers we will need and how to recruit and train them would have to wait.

At the moment I'm in no shape to decide anything. I'm cheerfully full of sweet wine and need to walk to the pot by the gate and take another piss. Then I'm going to crawl on to one of the string beds in the downstairs room of our little tower where the senior sergeants and original archers all sleep, except for Henry who sleeps with his woman. Yoram, of course, sleeps in the upstairs room with his family and our coins.

Tomorrow will be a busy day. We'll begin passing out the prize money for the Algerian prizes. Paying out the prize money could not be delayed even though we were still waiting for two of our galleys and five prizes to come in. We can't wait any longer. The men were promised their prize money when they got their prizes to Cyprus and many of them are already here. They need to be paid promptly or they'll start getting anxious.

Maybe when we finish handing out the prize coins, we'll have time to talk more about the additional archers––and, most important of all, where we'll find the additional archers to recruit and the longbows and pikes we'll need to properly equip them.

****** *William*

Bright and early the next morning, right after we've come back from pissing and visiting the shite hole, Yoram and I and the senior sergeants walked out of the tower to a horse cart waiting in the courtyard. I myself carried one of the sacks of coins over my shoulder and dropped it on the cart. Yoram carried the other, and Peter Sergeant and Richard Kent walked ahead of us wearing chain mail shirts and carrying swords. Peter was also carrying a sword for me along with his longbow and the two quivers of arrows and two bowstrings every archer is expected to have with him at all times.

Harold and the other senior sergeants were also wearing mail shirts and carrying their swords or bows. Even Yoram was wearing a chain shirt which, he explains a bit sheepishly, his wife made him put on even though he's not a fighting man.

Of course, we are ready to fight; one never knows what will happen when sacks of coins appear where everyone can see them and everyone knows they are coming.

It was my decision to pay out the men's prize money on the quay so everyone could see them get paid and our sailors and archers won't have to leave their cogs and galleys unattended to get their coins.

We could have, and perhaps should have, paid out the prize coins in private in the sergeants' courtyard. I decided to pay them out on the quay, however, because it is important for everyone to know we keep our word and pay what we owe.

Yoram had disagreed most respectfully last night when I announced the prize payments would be made on the quay in the morning. He was against paying out the prize coins where everyone could watch and only reluctantly agreed to participate. He was afraid robbers and pirates would be encouraged by seeing and hearing about all those coins to try to steal them and hurt his family in the process.

He may be right, but I think it is just as likely to have the reverse effect and I told him so—everyone will think we'll have no coins left after we pay out so many because that will be the story we'll once again tell to the local merchants when we next negotiate with them.

I guess we'll see.

In any event, Yoram seemed in good cheer despite my decision about paying the men in public and last night's heavy drinking. He smiled at me and moved forward to lead the horse after he dumped the sack he was carrying on to the cart next to mine.

He may be in good cheer but my head, on the other hand, is still a bit sore. But it was a bright sunny day and everyone we met was absolutely full of smiles and good cheer, so I soon recovered.

Everyone's cheerfulness as we followed the bouncing cart down the cart path to the beach was not surprising even though many of the onlookers are local men who were not on the raid and won't be sharing in the prize money. They were pleased because they could see we were keeping our word and intended to promptly pay what the men on the prize crews had been promised.

Being paid promptly and in full is very important to men who risk their lives for the coins they earn. Yoram and I know all too well what happens to those who don't pay fighting men what they are due. Indeed, that's how we met—when my brother killed the thieving bishop who tried not to pay us and we ended up with all of the bishop's many coins instead of only those we'd earned.

The bishop's greed got us started on our way up, didn't it?

A number of heavily armed senior sergeants fell in and walked with us as we came out of our little keep at sun-up and walk behind the horse cart towards the sergeant's gate. The sergeant's gate is the narrow gate in the original curtain wall. Only sergeants, no one else, are ever allowed through it into the little courtyard between the wall and the little stone farmhouse that is our keep.

The two-room farmhouse behind the wall is our compound's citadel. It's where Yoram and the important commanders and master sergeants, such as Harold and I and the original archers, live and where we keep our coin chests—Yoram and his family and coins in the room upstairs; the unmarried men of the survivors of the original archers and the other senior sergeants, such as Harold, in the room downstairs.

Only sergeants without women live in the courtyard between the tower and the first wall, where we are walking, and only the archers without women are allowed into the much larger courtyard between the first and second walls.

Similarly, only sergeants and archers with wives live between the second and the third wall that is still going up—to keep the sergeants and archers close and their women and children away from men's affairs and the coins.

Everyone else lives outside the new third wall—including our archers in training, sailors temporarily on shore, and the refugees and freed slaves. These people don't know it yet but many of them will be moving further out when Yoram starts building a fourth curtain wall. Then only the archers in training will be barracked between the third and fourth walls. *Defence in depth is what Thomas says the Romans called it. Or was that circumvallation? I forget.*

More and more men and women joined our parade as we moved through the baileys and down the cart path towards the beach. Everyone was cheerful and smiling, and there was much banter and waving and good cheer.

It's good to be alive and I'm very proud and trying not to show it.

****** *William*

Men and women were following us as we made our way to the Limassol quay where an even greater crowd was waiting. A line formed with the sergeant captains at the front, and then the prize captains, and then the sergeants and, finally, a long line other ranks.

Of course, the sergeant captains are first; rank has its privileges as Thomas says the Bible requires. Besides, after they're paid, we'll need the sergeant captains standing with us at the head of the line to make sure we make the proper payment when one of their men comes up.

It was a very long and very happy line.

"My God, Yoram, do we have enough coins?"

"Aye, William, we surely do—many more than enough with chests and chests to spare."

Yoram counted out the coins as Harold stood next to me to loudly announce to me what each man should be paid. And, of course, Harold and I thanked each and every one of them and shook his hand.

For some of the men it was quite an emotional and overwhelming day—they'd been slaves or serfs like me and Thomas and it was the first time they'd ever been paid coins or had their hand shaken by one of their superiors. For many, it was a big whoop of joy and they were off to the taverns and brothels or to the moneylenders standing nearby; for others, it was an abashed grin as a new wife standing in line with him promptly held out her hand before he could even turn away to find a bowl of ale.

I certainly hope the local barbers have a lot of herbs and medicines on hand and we don't lose too many men to the drips and pox.

Most of the crowd was dispersed by the time we finally finished passing out the prize coins and began to walk back to our stronghold with a couple of almost empty coin sacks. We were off to get something to eat from Thomas Cook at the kitchen and reminisce about days and friends gone by.

After I ate, I spent the afternoon with Brian and Henry to see what they are doing whilst Harold, Thomas, and Henry interview more of the slaves we took out of Algiers and the latest refugees. They needed to know what skills each man has and where we might use him. Some of those who want to stay will be assigned to training or work, others to the crews of our galleys and cogs.

In a day or two, when the assignments are complete, we'll begin sending the new galleys off to the Holy Land ports and the cogs to fish for pirates. We're going to begin regular visits to more ports now that we have so many galleys.

Chapter Seven
Another source of coins.

We'd finished paying out the prize money and were on our way to Thomas Cook's kitchen in the outer bailey, when who should show up and be standing there with big smiles on their faces and outstretched hands to be shaken, but a group of merchants including Aaron from here in Limassol and several men I'd met before but definitely didn't expect to ever see again—Aaron's friend Reuben from Latika and two of the merchants I'd met in Alexandria whose names I could never pronounce in the first place.

Our plans for eating and spending the afternoon changed when it turned out they'd come all this way to welcome me back to Cyprus and invite me to eat and drink with them and several of their fellow merchants. The intensity of their invitation suggested they had something else they wanted to talk about and it was important.

Hopefully, it isn't that Latika has fallen and is no longer a refuge for Christians and Jews fleeing the

Saracens. Latika can't be it; we have men and galleys constantly visiting there. Yoram would have told me immediately if Latika had fallen.

******

The merchants enthusiastically invited everyone, so Harold and Yoram and Henry came with me to the merchants' meal, and so did Peter Sergeant and Richard Kent. It was a great meal with endless dishes and it went on for the entire afternoon.

Peter and Richard don't say a word. This was their first visit outside to Cyprus and they were wide-eyed and clearly astounded by the variety of things available in the Limassol market and all the different foods set in front of us—just as Thomas and I were last year.

Last year seems like ages ago, in another life; aye, that it does.

We talked of our families and our health and many other things before the real reason for the merchants' request for a meeting finally came out. And, of course, one of the things we talk about is the old quarries for the perfectly understandable reason of our wanting to use them to get the stone we need to face our new log walls. We needed more and we'd already mined all the old ruins we could find.

"They're copper and limestone mines from the olden days of the Romans," suggested Reuben.

"They were shut down long ago when iron began replacing bronze. Probably during the time of the

Romans, when the island ran out of trees to make the charcoal which has to be burned to cook the ore. They're useless now. You ought to be able to get them off King Guy for a song—he's greedy, the Frenchman is. Always trying to raise our taxes, isn't he?"

Copper? Copper can go with tin to make coins, can't it?

"Uh, Reuben. What do you know about the old mines—are any of them still operating?"

"They've all been closed for a long time. I doubt anyone even knows when they were last worked or who worked them. It was probably the Romans."

****** *William*

I learnt a lot from the merchants before they finally brought forth what they wanted to talk about. They want us to place a galley in Latika permanently and establish a defendable compound with a strong force of defenders, a place where their families can temporarily gather to escape by sea.

And, "oh yes, and what do you think about us opening trading posts all along the coast of the Holy Land and acting as your agents to book cargos and passengers?"

Ah. That's it for sure. They've seen the coins we're earning and want a slice.

"That would be quite dangerous for you, wouldn't it? Opening trading compounds all along the coast, I mean."

"Yes, but quite lucrative for everyone including

you and your company of men. And our agents and their families would be able to escape on your galleys if the Saracens come."

The merchants brought a very specific proposal—they will put an agent with his own defendable walled compound in every port still in Christian or Jewish hands including Constantinople, Antioch, and Beirut.

They even waved their hands about and suggested they might even be able to do so in some of the ports the Saracens have taken, such as Aleppo—and even possibly inland in cities such as Damascus and Jerusalem.

In essence, our archers would be the compound guards and row them and their families to safety on a galley standing by just as we now are prepared to do for the merchants in Acre and Alexandria.

Constantinople, Beirut, and the smaller Christian ports I can understand. But the Saracen port of Aleppo, and inland at Damascus and Jerusalem? Impossible.

"Aleppo, Damascus, and Jerusalem? Forgive me, but the Saracens control those cities. Your proposals are hard for me to understand."

Or believe.

"Yes, but we think we can put agents in those cities if we use Saracen or Jewish guards instead of your archers. They may be controlled by the Saracens but trade is trade as you well know—and you English have fearsome reputations for protecting your galleys and whatever they carry.

"Your reputation is important," he said. "It's why more and more of the merchants and landlords are paying to send some of their coins here for you to hold for them. They are much safer here with you than in Syria and Egypt."

Damn, he's right—and if everyone knows about the coins we have here we're in real danger from an attack by the King or pirates. Worse, the danger will grow if we expand our trade.

"Well, some of what you said is not quite accurate. You do know, I hope, we deliberately keep very few of our coins here on Cyprus. We are fully aware of the danger of attracting robbers and pirates—so the coins we receive are either immediately spent or quickly sent on to England. We send them on fast and heavily armed galleys and bring them back only when they are needed to meet our obligations."

That's not exactly true but it will be soon.

****** *William*

I sobered up a bit on the walk back to our camp. Then Harold, Henry, Yoram, and I spent the rest of the evening talking about the merchants' proposal. Yoram likes it. He thinks the idea of having the merchants act as our agents is a good idea, but only if they don't get too big a share of the coins. He made a very persuasive argument.

"We now have enough galleys to serve the ports and cities where the merchants want to be our agents— but we don't have enough men who can scribe and sum to operate in those ports by ourselves. And if we don't start serving them someone else will, probably the

Venetians."

Cyprus, Yoram suggested with a great deal of enthusiasm, could be the centre of our activities in the Holy Land with the merchants acting as our agents until we find men of our own to take the merchants' places.

We talked late into the night and a conclusion was reached. Yoram's enthusiasm carried the day; if the merchants will agree to our terms, we'll stick to the sea and let them operate as our agents in most of the Holy Land and Egyptian ports. We'll also agree to continue stationing escape galleys in ports where the merchants pay a sufficiently large annual fee. *Though, how we might provide an escape galley for the merchants and notables of inland cities such as Aleppo and Damascus is quite beyond me.*

But we won't use the merchants as agents in Acre and Alexandria where we already have posts and never in Rome, Beirut, Antioch, and Constantinople—which are too big and too important to leave to anyone else. We'll operate in those cities ourselves with our own sergeants and our own compounds and guards.

Yoram was particularly adamant we maintain total control of whatever we decide to do at Constantinople. He thinks the crusade now forming in Europe will go there first and there will be many rich crusaders willing to pay to be taken to Constantinople and many rich refugees willing to pay to flee from them.

That's very interesting. Thomas heard similar rumours about Constantinople from the papal nuncio in London. It seems the crusaders have asked the Pope for permission to go to the Holy Land via Constantinople. It doesn't make sense, does it? Travelling via Constantinople was understandable in the first two crusades when the crusaders marched overland to Jerusalem. So why would the crusaders want to go there now if they will be travelling to the Holy Land by sea in order to avoid Saladin's lands in Kurdistan?

"Yoram, have you heard why the crusaders might go out of their way and stop at Constantinople? It's out of the way if they intend to sail from Venice instead of walk; it doesn't make sense."

****** *William*

Early the next morning, I send word to Aaron and Reuben and told them Yoram, Harold, Henry, and I would like to meet with them again to talk about their proposal. I suggested we meet at Reuben's market stall once again for another meal.

Why not? The food is good. But this time I will be drinking sweetened tea instead of celebrating my safe arrival and drinking wine. It's very good tea, you know—very sweet.

Chapter Eight
Surprise arrivals and new ideas.

One of the two galleys I'd left in England rowed into harbour this morning with messages and a couple of parchment money orders—and who should be on it, in command, but Bob Farmer with Little Mathew as his chosen man. And they're not the only ones who returned to re-join the company after going home for a visit.

Bob and Mathew had all kinds of news and brought me a long parchment letter from Thomas. It seems Andrew Brewer also returned to Falmouth looking for us and so did Alan the smith and a number of the English refugees and slaves we'd carried back to England.

Most of the returning archers are at Restormel with Thomas and he reported that he'd been using them to good effect. He's got some of them putting the learning on our new recruits to be archers and how to fight with our long-bladed pikes; the refugees and freed slaves who returned are either working on a new wall for Restormel or helping in the smithy or brewery or stables.

Thomas's parchment gave me a twinge of

homesickness. He reported George was healthy and doing splendidly even though I'm not there, his school now has nine boys plus George learning to scribe and gobble church talk, and there has not been a peep out of Earl of Devon.

Thomas believes our victory over FitzCount and his men has caused what's left of the local manor holders, both the two remaining knights and the handful of franklins, to pull back and count their blessings they weren't there to die with him. They are, he wrote, beginning to come in to meet and greet and their rather modest rents and taxes seem to be coming in normally.

"I wave my cross at them as your representative and tell them you're a fair man and you'll leave them alone if they behave themselves and stay loyal and pledge their liege. If not, I tell them you're a hard man and it's into the river for them with their bollocks missing and no prayers when you throw them in."

Thomas reported that he has not yet told them to free their serfs and make them into tenants. That's coming, he wrote, but he wants me there with more archers when the order is given—in case anyone rises in rebellion and brings in their friends and relatives from outside Cornwall.

What he is also doing is once again sending some of our men out into the English countryside as recruiting sergeants to find boys for his school. They do it at the same time they pass the word we are looking for archers and men with strong arms willing to become apprentice archers.

"We want bright village lads capable of learning to scribe and sum, not the lads of the knights and nobles."

Our recruiting sergeants are told to say those exact words about the boys we are seeking. The recruiting sergeants are also acting as spies and talking to the local priests and the men they recruit to see if anyone is organising against us.

That's very smart of Thomas; the priests know everything and they love to talk. It's a pity there are so few of them left.

****** *William*

Our second meeting with the merchants went well. Yoram, Henry, and Harold came with me and we spent the entire afternoon hammering out a detailed agreement for all the ports on the coast of the Holy Land except Antioch and Acre. We finally ended up agreeing we'd talk about them later when we see how well everything works out at the other ports.

Basically, we agreed to station as many evacuation galleys in whatever ports the merchants specify for the same yearly price and terms per galley the merchants are now paying at Acre; the merchants will also have an agent secretly representing us in Damascus and Jerusalem and openly at each port they decide to serve on the coast of the Holy Land and elsewhere except for Constantinople and any other ports we reserve to ourselves.

It was a good contract for the merchants—they will receive a fee of one coin of every ten we receive for carrying the passengers, cargo, and money order parchments they arrange.

Included in the contract was our right to closely question every passenger and cargo recipient as to how much he paid for our services. Also included was the right of the sergeant captains of our galleys to refuse to carry any passenger or cargo or money payment order. What was not written on the parchment was my verbal promise to immediately kill any of their agents who attempt to cheat us.

"You won't have to come back to do that," Aaron assured me as the other merchants nodded grimly. "Because they will already be dead."

******

Today four prizes taken by one of our cogs arrived one after another. Then Albert's cog came in by itself to collect its prize money and take on a new company of archers for another trip. It was a big day for Albert and he was beaming as he stood with me and Yoram on the quay whilst we paid his men and shook their hands.

Later in day, the other pirate-taking cog, William Chester's, also came in with a totally different tale to tell—William ran into a great pirate fleet of more than twenty Moorish galleys off Alexandria and almost didn't escape. Only his archers saved him and almost ran out of arrows in the process.

There's a lesson to be learnt from William Chester's experience according to Harold—our galleys and cogs need to sail with more bales of arrows and more archers on board. Yoram and I promptly authorised Brian to spend coins to employ more fletchers and smiths, and I ordered Cornwall to recruit more archer apprentices and step up everyone's training. As soon as possible, we'll only send our archers to sea—if they are both archers and swordsmen. We definitely need more short swords and small shields and longbows, in addition to more of the new bladed pikes our smiths are producing.

******

The days that followed were filled with preparing our galleys and cogs for their new assignments and training the men who will sail in them. We had the galleys and sailors we needed to provide more cargo and passenger services to the Holy Land ports, but we were woefully short of qualified archers and longbows for them to use.

Henry got a good response when he issued a recruiting call among the refugees and the slaves we brought in from Algiers and from Albert's five prizes. But even if every one of them qualifies as an archer, which is not at all likely since it requires a good eye and a pair of very strong arms for a man to hold a nocked arrow to his chest and push out a longbow, we'll still be short of both men and longbows.

I immediately began marshalling and reassigning our men to adjust to our new arrangement with the merchants. One of my first moves was to recall our senior sergeants from Acre and Alexandria so the merchants can take over their duties.

Yes, after thinking it over, I decided to let the merchants also have Alexandria. I need to use Randolph elsewhere—Constantinople, I should think.

Based on what the merchants are telling us, it looks like we'll have eight of our galleys and their crews under contract for merchant evacuations. In addition, we'll need to have at least one each in Constantinople, Beirut, and Antioch to evacuate our own people and at least two each in Cyprus and England for training and messenger purposes.

Those commitments and the new prizes mean we'll have thirty-three galleys available for our own use—and the list does not include one of our galleys which is more than a week overdue and may have somehow been lost or taken.

We also have six cogs of which four are available to carry prize-takers or cargo, the old leaky cog we bought in Larnaca is in Cyprus as a training cog, and Harold's battered, old pirate-taker is still not fully repaired due to the lack of appropriate wood and qualified boat wrights.

Thirty-three galleys plus whatever Moorish galleys the cogs sailing as pirate-takers bring us in the future should give us more than enough galleys if they all sail shorthanded in order to carry the maximum number of passengers. Also we need to switch our galley yard to building bigger galleys and cogs with higher sides and archer shooting slits for our own use. Not being able to take the big three-master in Algiers was a real eye-opener.

******   *William*

We agreed. Yoram will go to the King's summer palace at Famagusta to see the King's chamberlain about the mines and the big trees, and I will stay in Limassol and write a parchment for one of our galleys to carry to Thomas. I need to bring him up to date about our raid on Algiers and let him know of the changes we need to make, particularly the need to recruit more apprentice archers.

I thought about going to Famagusta myself or with Yoram to visit the King's chancellor, but Yoram and Henry were dead set against it. They feared we'd both be taken by King Guy for ransom, or worse.

I decided not to go with Yoram after a lot of discussion with my senior sergeants and some casual conversations with Aaron and the local merchants, who warned against it—so I could mount a rescue effort or provide a credible threat if one became necessary.

Most important among our problems was our desperate shortage of archers to crew the additional galleys and cogs we took out of Algiers. Accordingly, in my parchment to Thomas, I asked him to send out as many recruiting parties as possible and to make a major effort to recruit and train longbow archers and buy longbows and yew wood for our recruits and bow-makers.

Wales, I suggested, might be a good place to

recruit more archers and buy yew for bows if he couldn't find enough in England.

They're tough little buggers up there in Wales, you know. Richard had several companies of them.

I also suggested, if we carried through with our plan to set up a boatyard in Cornwall in the spring, it should build big cogs with two or three masts such as we could not take in Algiers because its sides were so high above our galley. And, of course, I reminded him he should always thoroughly search the ballast space in every arriving galley for one of Yoram's chests.

We're going to send a chest of coins in the ballast of every galley and cog we send to England; it will be a secret—we'll install it and then put on an all-new crew of sailors and archers.

Scribing all I wanted to tell to Thomas required several big parchments—because after I finished describing our immediate needs, I began writing about the old copper and limestone mines here on Cyprus and reminded him we have access to charcoal and tin in Cornwall and cogs and galleys capable of carrying them as ballast or cargo in either direction.

Thomas has a good head; he'll know I'm also talking about coins without having to mention them in case the parchment falls into the wrong hands.

I suggested it might be a good idea when he sends out his recruiting parties for some of them to go where they might also be able to recruit men who know how to use their hands such as tailors and coiners "who could be taught to use such materials to make metal arrowheads and such."

Thomas is smart; he'll understand what I'm thinking about when he sees my mention of coiners.

And that raised a question for which we needed answers before we could start making arrowheads and coins—would it be easier to bring the tin and coal or charcoal to the copper and iron mines or the copper and iron ore to the tin and coal mines? And where should we do it, and how do we cope with the fact that we have no silver or iron mines?

****** *Yoram*

My trip to Famagusta to meet with the King's chamberlain took five rather leisurely days. But it wasn't a hard trip because I had a horse to ride and we had a horse cart carrying our tents and food. I suppose I could have gone by galley but I wanted to see the land. Most of the men walked and I mostly walked with them after my arse became quite sore from all the bouncing and rubbing.

The only thing hard was leaving Lena and Aria. Truth be told? I was glad to get away for a few days.

Our arrival at Famagusta's main city gate was expected and we were promptly admitted. I had, after all, sent a parchment from Limassol last week saying I would be coming to see the chancellor, Lord Alstain, to discuss buying some of the King's trees and the abandoned mines. Our troubles began as soon as we passed through the city gate and dismounted—we were promptly surrounded by a large group of the king's guards and disarmed.

After our horses and cart were led away, we were marched to a low stone building, which is apparently some kind of guard house or prison. It was a foul place because its previous occupants stayed here long enough to piss and shite all over the place. Our reception was very worrisome and my men were extremely upset, and so was I.

I finally began shouting for Lord Alstain. He didn't come. Instead, a group of armed men appeared and dragged me off to a very dark and wet cell. And then to make things worse, I had to shite and there was no bowl of water to use to wipe my arse.

Oh my god. No one knows I'm here.

Finally, a man I've never seen before opened the door and walked in holding his nose. He was wearing a sword and a couple of armed men behind him were standing at the door.

"You are the man called Yoram who is in command of the pirates camping at Limassol?"

Chapter Nine

Yoram has been taken.

"I'm getting worried, Henry. We should have heard from Yoram by now."

Two hours later, Aaron hurried in all out of breath and I discovered I had a great deal to worry about. Merchants on a cog from Famagusta had just arrived and were reporting Yoram has been arrested and thrown into the castle's dungeon. What they didn't know is why.

I ran a quick count in my mind as to how many men we have in port who I can immediately marshal into a relief force. Then I sent Peter and Richard running to round up the senior sergeants so I could give them the news and their marching orders.

It would seem we've got just under two thousand men in port of which at least a thousand are fully trained as archers and perhaps five hundred more who are apprentice archers and capable of being pike men. We've also got about three hundred sailors.

King Guy is thought to have about three thousand

men pledged to him, but they're scattered all over the island and many of them are barely trained and poorly armed. And we'll be getting stronger and stronger as more and more of our galleys return in the normal course of our operations.

I was angry with myself for letting Yoram go and for not knowing more about the King's forces. I was also beside myself with fury—finishing off whoever is responsible for this is going to be as enjoyable as eating a piece of warm bread slathered with fresh butter. The only thing certain is those who are responsible are going to die terrible deaths if Yoram or any of the men with him are tortured or killed.

Thomas Cook and Harold were the first to arrive. Henry came in right behind them. They knew something's up from the serious look on my face and what little they might have been told by Peter or Richard.

"Bad news, my friends. Yoram and his men have been taken for ransom by the King. We, of course, are going to marshal our forces and try to rescue them even if it means killing that jumped-up French bastard."

"Thomas, we'll need to feed up to two thousand men every day for an unlimited period of time in Famagusta instead of here in Limassol. Work with Aaron and your local suppliers to have them deliver food to the quay instead of here starting immediately. We'll move the supplies to Famagusta by galley.

"Henry and I going leave immediately with as many archers as Brian can provide with pikes so the archers can land with two ranks of pikes in case they hit us with knights. We'll back them up with three ranks of archers.

"Harold, you'll stay and be in command here with Bob Farmer as your second in charge of defending our citadel and Thomas Cook as your second in charge of getting our supplies. It means you've got two things to do.

"One is to stay here and guard the compound with Bob and our apprentice archers in training; the other is to make sure our galleys and cogs bring us the rest of our archers and the supplies Thomas and Brian get to the quay.

"We'll be in Famagusta as long as it takes—I won't be back until I either have Yoram and our men safe or the head and guts of the men responsible."

I'm so furious I could pop a blood channel or fall down in a fit.

"Oh yes, and I'll be sailing on the lead galley myself without any pikes."

Then I explained to Harold why the first galley was to have no pikes and asked him to assign me the best galley captain and crew he's got in port who's likely to help me pull it off. He's also to add the ten best swordsmen we've got among the men now in Limassol to the first galley's crew even if they are also archers.

****** *William*
It took me longer than I would have thought to marshal our forces and get the initial galleys underway.

We have a problem—we have the archers we need on hand and we have men trained to walk in step and use the pikes, but we only have a little more than three hundred or so of the long-handled bladed pikes Brian has been producing.

And good pikes they are too—Brian's smiths have added a hooked blade about a foot below their metal points.

What we do have, thanks to Henry and his sergeants, are archers who have been trained to use both longbows and pikes and also trained to fight and walk together on land to the beat of a rowing drum. The pike men do the rowing and boarding at sea and are paid as apprentice archers until they qualify with longbows.

And they ought to be well trained. It was Henry himself who came up with the idea of our archers fighting on land in five lines with the first two being sword-wearing and shield-carrying pike men to hold off the mounted knights with their pikes followed by three lines of shield-carrying archers to kill everyone in front of the pikes. Hopefully, it will work as well here on Cyprus as it worked in Cornwall at Bossiney. It should—if we have enough pikes.

****** *Yoram*

A warder just looked through the peephole of my cell and was opening the door. "Lord Alstain is here to see you," he announced with a sneer. The warder's a bald man with a big red birthmark on his forehead.

The King's chancellor was all business and

arrogant beyond belief. He's heard about the chests of coins in our compound and he wants them "for the King."

I wonder how he found out about our coin chests. No one is allowed up the steps except me and Lena. He probably assumes it's where I would keep our coins because it's the safest place. Well, he's right about that.

"Your choice is to order them turned over to me or to stay here and die of starvation and a lack of water. It's your choice."

I know I need to play for time, so I pretended to be very bitter and resigned—which wasn't hard to do under the circumstances.

"I can see I have no choice and I certainly don't want to die. So I'll pay the ransom even though Lord William will probably kill me when he finds out.

"But you know, of course, that the men I left in Limassol will not trust whatever your messenger tells them. They'll pay our ransom if I tell them to pay it, but, without a doubt, before they do they'll send someone to see if I really did send the message and that my men and I are still alive and being treated properly."

Alstain doesn't seem to know that William is here on Cyprus. I wonder what he will do; William, that is.

Chapter Ten
Organizing a rescue.

The sun was going down as the first seven of our galleys rowed out of the harbour and began a high-speed voyage along the coast of the island to Famagusta with all the men I could initially muster. If we row hard all night and swap off rowers every couple of hours we should get to Famagusta sometime tomorrow depending on the weather and winds—hopefully that will be at least two or three days before the King expects us, if he expects us at all.

Two or three days early, that is, if the King expects us to march to Famagusta like soldiers instead of coming by sea.

****** *William*

Our first galley, the one I was on, entered the Famagusta harbour well ahead of the other six under Henry's command and the dozen or more following along behind Henry's first six.

Henry and his men were hugging the coast east of the Famagusta harbour entrance and out of sight—and waiting temporarily whilst a young archer counted off five thousand marching steps on the deck of his galley. That's how long I'd given my men and myself to walk through the city gate serving the quay and into the walled city.

No one on the quay paid much attention when our galley rowed up in the intense summer heat and a couple of men jumped off and nonchalantly moored it to a couple of the quay's mooring posts. Then more men got off. One or two were carrying bows slung over their shoulders but none of them were carrying swords and shields or wearing helmets.

In other words, we looked like normal sailors bringing cargo to the merchants in the city's market from a galley—nothing out of the ordinary to bother anyone on a hot summer's day, unless, of course, he happened to notice the bows were strung and the tunics of some of the men were covering chain mail shirts despite the heat.

One reason the men looked so harmless as they trudged up to the city wall from the quay is because the men who got off the galley were in four-man teams of cargo carriers and each team was carrying a pallet of cargo into the city through the gate serving the city's market.

The pallets are actually cut down ladders from the construction underway on our third wall and the cargos under the rough linen covers are swords and quivers of arrows and more longbows.

There were a couple of sleepy guards standing in the shade near the gate who tried to wave the first four men to a stop. But the cargo carriers smiled and nodded their heads and said something in English which was a foreign language the guards didn't understan—and kept right on going towards the market and its stalls. They even ignored a somewhat shouted command to stop.

The cargo carriers following them kept on coming as well and also walked right on past the guards without slowing or stopping.

It wasn't until the fourth or fifth team of cargo carriers passed through the gate and kept on walking that one of the guards began to get suspicious. He walked out into the hot sunlight and grabbed a passing cargo carrier by the arm to stop him. He was shrugged off and the man kept walking.

The alarm wasn't raised until the gate guard made the mistake of pulling back the cloth covering the weapons of the next cargo litter, and then jumping back and shouting a warning.

It was a serious mistake and just about the last thing the gate guard ever did—because one of the cargo carriers, me, promptly dropped the corner of the cargo litter he was carrying and cut the guard's throat with a thrust of the knife concealed in his tunic sleeve.

I did it so quickly the end of the cargo litter didn't even have time to hit the ground before I took him. The guard just stood there in shocked disbelief after he grabbed his throat and looked at the blood pouring out over his hands.

The men at the end of our long line of sweating cargo carriers trudging toward the gate in the sun heard the guard's warning and my loudly shouted order to hurry. They began running and so did the other guard. The difference being that the "cargo carriers" were running for the gate and the guard was running away.

More and more of the sweating cargo carriers rushed into the city after the alarm was raised—until we were all in and we shut and barred the gate behind us.

We're in, by God!

****** *William*

Weapons were snatched off the cargo litters, and a few seconds later more than a hundred heavily armed and terribly overheated swordsmen and archers were running through Famagusta's narrow streets on an incredibly hot summer afternoon.

We were running for the castle gate on the other side of the walled city, the gate which opens on to the cart path leading up to the King's castle.

Before we left Limassol, Henry and Harold found several former slaves who knew the city and brought them to me. They led us in a great puffing and gasping run along the cobblestoned streets to the city gate opposite the King's castle on the hill above the city.

It was not an easy run. One of our men suddenly stopped and fainted and fell down on the hot cobblestones. A little later, another stopped and leaned against a wall with a pain in his side; we continued on without them. We didn't even slow down.

As I followed our guides around a corner where the street turned, I could see a small group of men up ahead of me at another gate in the city wall. Several men who may or may not have been guards were standing in the shade near the gate. They were obviously alerted by the shouts that followed us and the chattering sound of so many sandals slapping on the cobblestones as we ran towards them.

The men at the gate looked intently towards us for a few seconds—and then they too decided to run. It's a good thing they did; we were much too tired to fight. At least I was. It's damn hot running in the sun of a summer afternoon on Cyprus.

Famagusta is a big city, almost ten thousand people. It took a while to run all the way through the city to reach the castle gate on the other side. By the time I got there, my legs were aching and tired and I was sweating like a pig and totally out of breath, and so were the men who were running with me.

I watched and listened as the escaping and shouting guards ran up the cart track to the castle whilst I was bent over with my hands on my knees trying to catch my breath.

Well, it won't be long now before the alarm really sounds. I wonder what it will be? Church bells probably. I wonder what the King will do?

The men running away to the castle were not the only ones scared into action. There weren't many people on the streets because the heat virtually shuts down Cyprus's cities every summer afternoon. But those who did see us watched with dismay and growing alarm as our big group of heavily armed and sweating men lumbered past.

There were a few shouted questions, but no one waited to ask questions as we hurried past—children were shooed inside by anxious women, men dove into doorways, and, all over the city, doors and gates started being barred and merchant stalls began closing.

We quickly shut the gate in the city wall leading to the King's castle and left several dozen men to guard it. Then we lumbered off to the other city gates and repeated the process. Only when all the gates into the city were closed and barred did we begin hunting down whatever was left of the King's men in the city. There weren't many and they quickly surrendered.

****** *William*

The last gate in Famagusta's city wall was being shut and barred by my exhausted men as Henry's galleys arrived and began rapidly unloading their men on to the quay.

So far there has been absolutely no resistance. The King and his men were in the castle up above the city and by now they almost certainly knew something was wrong even though they probably didn't know what it was.

One of our men ran up some stone steps to the top of the city wall and shouted down the news of our galleys arrival. They are, he reported, unloading at the quay. I ran up the steps two at time to see for myself. *Water. I need water.*

Then I stood sweating in the shade of a stone pillar and watched Henry's men as they poured off their galleys and formed up into a fighting column. It was quite impressive.

And I was certainly glad that the man who trained them is with the first of the forces I was marshalling here.

Within minutes after it moored, each galley was emptied of its men and began heading back to Limassol to pick up more men and supplies. It would take each of the galleys quite a bit longer to get back to Limassol since a goodly number of the rowers who got it here so quickly were among the archers and pike men forming up into their ranks and columns on the quay.

A drum began beating as each galley's company of archers finished forming up into its ranks. Then the men began marching off the quay with all of them stepping together to the beat of their company's drum just as they pulled their oars together when they were rowing to it.

I don't know why, but it impresses me every time I see men marching together like that.

****** *William*

Evan was the sergeant captain of the galley whose men were the first to get into the city. He's a Welshman, one of the archers we recruited in Acre. He served in one of Richard's English-speaking companies of archers and learnt enough English to get by.

Henry and Harold selected Evan and his crew to go into the city with me, so they must think he and his men are capable. And so far he's been proving to be a very good choice.

Evan and I had several long talks on the galley coming here, so I was fairly sure he knew what he and his men were expected to do once we got into the city. He's got a former galley slave with him who speaks Greek in case he needs an interpreter for the local citizens.

In any event, Henry's men were starting to march up from the quay so it's time for me to join them; so I shook Evan's hand and congratulated him on a job well done. Then I took Peter and Richard and the ten swordsmen in my personal force and started walking back to the gate which opens to the cart path running up from the quay.

Evan and his men did a good job of getting us into the city. They need to be recognised; I wonder if he'd be a good man to be in charge of an office in Beirut if we can find an acceptable scribe to do his writing and sums.

Famagusta was extremely quiet as my fetchers and swordsmen and I walked back to the gate in the city walls serving the quay. No one was about. And that was a pity for I was terribly thirsty. I would have dearly loved to have had a drink of water or ale or some fruit to eat—and I'm sure the men felt the same.

A dozen or so of the men from Evan's crew watched as we approach the city gate reached by the cart path from the quay. They were ranged against the city wall in an effort to escape the relentless sun. Several more were up on wall standing in what little shade there is up there. They were watching the quay and the cart track leading up to the gate.

"Well done, lads, well done. We've got the city and so far no one's been hurt except one of theirs," I said to the waiting archers as I walked up to them and pointed to the guard with the cut throat who is still lying on the ground near the gate. *Things have been going well elsewhere in the city as well and they needed to know it.*

"We're going out, lads. Bar the gate after we leave and guard it with your lives. Don't let anyone except our own men in. No exceptions no matter what they say or promise."

With that, we unbarred the gate and started down towards the quay. When we got part way down, I realised Henry's main force was marching up from the quay towards us. So I stopped and waited. *No sense in getting any more hot and thirsty than we already are.*

"Hello, Henry," I shouted from off to the side of the track as the first of his men come marching past to the beat of their company's rowing drum.

"Your men look impressive, very impressive. Did you hear the city is ours without losing a single man?"

I want the men Henry trained to know these things.

When Henry reached me, he explained he was coming this way because the fastest way for him to get his men to the King's castle was to march them through the city's streets and lanes.

"Good thinking, Henry. Good thinking."

****** *William*

My little company of men joined Henry's march through the city and I walked with him so we could talk. Because it was the shortest route to the King's castle, all of our companies would march through the city on their way there.

More and more people came out to look as our companies marched past to the beat of their booming drums—and more and more of them began clapping and waving as they realised where we were headed. The new Roman Catholic French king imposed by the Templars was not exactly popular with his Greek-speaking subjects, most of whom were members of the Orthodox Church.

We passed through the city's castle gate, and Henry himself led the first four of our archer companies to positions just out of arrow range in front of the castle's main gate. We could be wrong, of course, but it is likely this is where a sortie will come if there is one.

The last two companies coming through the gate marched off to their positions elsewhere around the castle. They'll take up similar positions in front of each of the castle's two smaller side doors each day and remain there until darkness falls. Then they too will come join us in front of the castle's main gate.

My plan was simple—absolutely no one would be allowed to leave or enter the castle until Yoram and our men are released, not if we can help it at least. What we didn't know was how much food and water was in the castle or if there were any secret entrances.

Actually, that's not true—we'll let women and children leave so as to not upset the people in the city. Only the King and his men will starve until our men are released.

****** *William*

As our men marched to their positions, each file of five men used their left hands to help carry two of Brian's special pikes with a cutting blade and hook about a foot short of its metal point. Carrying them in such a manner resulted in each file of five men standing in a very straight line as well as being shoulder to shoulder with the file on either side of it.

Hopefully, carrying their pikes thusly also means the men in the castle will not see the pikes and realise what they are until they are raised—and then it will be too late, much too late.

Henry told his men to "stand at ease" and "use your water skins" as he and I walked past the four company formations to inspect them.

That's when we realised our first mistake.

It was much too hot for our men to stand out here in the sun. A few men from each company were given coins from Henry's purse and sent back into the city to buy fruit and water.

Indeed, it was so hot we didn't wait for them to return—a few minutes later, Henry ordered his companies to fall back to the city wall and sit in the shade. Then we waited.

We didn't have to wait very long. Suddenly, the gate in the castle's curtain wall opened and an elderly priest began walking down the cart track towards us. Henry and I stood up and walked out to meet him.

"Greetings, brothers. King Guy wants to know who you are and why you are here."

My response was very cold and very menacing.

"I am the Earl of Cornwall and I am here to fetch my men who are being held by the King for ransom. And I will be here with my army until I either get my men back safely—or I get the heads of every man responsible, and coins for my trouble and for my men's trouble, including yours and the King's."

Whilst I was telling the priest my terms, he was obviously counting how many men we have. He was such a dunce he was moving his lips as he counted.

He's probably not a priest at all; I wonder if I should kill him?

"I will, of course, pass Your Lordship's request to His Majesty."

"It's not a request," I snarled in the most vicious voice I could manage.

"You can tell the King that I either get my men immediately or I'll wait right here until he starves and take all the coins and all the heads in his castle— including his and yours."

The priest was aghast as he listened but merely nodded and said he'd give the King my message. Then he turned and trudged back up the hill.

The sun passed overhead and went down without there being any response to my very just demands.

Chapter Eleven
King Guy's attack.

We were munching on our bread and cheese in the cool
of the early morning and the sun was still behind the
castle towering above us when the castle gate opened and
a large force of mounted knights and running men came
hurrying out. They obviously intended to form up and
come straight down the hill at us.

There was a great shout and lots of pointing from
the archers when the castle gate began opening. All
around me men began stringing their bows and checking
their arrows to make sure they were laid out properly.

We were expecting some sort of sortie. It was
inevitable we'd be tested to see if we were really a
serious threat. That's why we slept and ate in our ranks
and have been standing to arms since long before the sun
came up.

Even so, the sudden appearance of the King's
men was a surprise and there was a lot of shouting and
running about as everyone hurried to his place.

The King's men would have the benefit of the
relatively steep downward slope of the castle hill and

their ability to determine when they are going to attack and where they will hit our line.

We have something going for us too—battle experience and the long days of intense training and our new bladed pikes and our longbows—the new weapons the King's French knights and their soldiers were unlikely to have ever faced before.

I like our chances; yes, I do.

Henry gave the orders and the sergeants repeated them as they'd done so many times before in practise.

"Prepare to push lights and then heavies when they come in range," the sergeants began to cry. The sergeants' cries changed to, "Pike men kneel and prepare to set your pikes," when the mounted men began moving down the hill towards us.

We were closed up in five, tight, shoulder-to-shoulder lines with no gaps between our six companies when the pikes were readied and our archers nocked their arrows. The first two lines were pike men and they were close upon one another. There was no question about it—our front would bristle with pikes like the quills of a hedgehog when the pikes were raised.

Each of the three lines of archers behind the pike men were six paces back from the line in front of them, so every archer would have enough room to lay his arrows and sword on his shield lying in front of him and room to shoot.

When the order was given, every archer would initially begin pushing out his lighter arrows to get the greatest distance and then switch to his heavier armour-piercing arrows when the King's men get in range.

It was the heavy arrows which could punch right through the armour of king's knights and men-at-arms; the light ones can get the horses and the men's unarmoured parts and fly one hundred or more paces farther than the heavies depending on the strength of the archer's push.

Coming out of our longbows both types of arrows fly faster and harder and at least several hundred paces further than similar arrows shot by regular bows.

******

Guy and his knights may have heard about longbows and bladed pikes, but they had obviously never faced them. As they come out of the gate, they moved down the slope towards the city walls and began to form up where the King or whoever was in command thought they would be safely out of arrow range. Bad mistake. We've got longbows and they were forming up well within what we called "our killing land."

Mounted knights and fast-walking foot soldiers were still coming out of the castle gate and beginning to form up for their charge when Henry shouted his order and it was loudly repeated through our ranks by every sergeant and chosen man.

"Notch lights. Constant launch. PUSH. Constant launch. PUSH."

Four hundred archers immediately began dropping a continuous hailstorm of arrows on the King's men, trying to form up in front of the castle's gate. They raised their shields, of course, but there was consternation and confusion in their ranks as more and more men and horses were hit.

Then the King or whoever was in command lost his head in response to the rain of arrows. He made another mistake—instead of moving back to get out of range, he ordered a charge even before the last of his men was out of the castle's gate.

The knights who were still on their horses, and most of them still were despite our initial rain of arrows, began galloping down the hill to attack us with their infantry support coming behind them and falling further and further back.

Our archers instinctively turned their aim towards the oncoming horsemen. The knights were coming particularly fast because their horses were fresh and they were charging downhill.

The charge of the King's riders through the heavy rain of arrows resulted in more and more horses and knights going down—and when they did, they often took others down with them when their horses stumbled over a fallen rider or horse.

Less than a minute after the arrows began flying and the charge started, about twenty of the King's mounted men finally reached our lines and the pikes waiting for them.

Most of the charging horsemen who reached us had their visors down and never even saw the pikes on which their horses were about to be impaled. A few of them saw our pikes come up and tried to turn away at the last moment when they realised what it meant. None succeeded.

The knights and horses who survived our arrow storm ran straight on to our line of heavy pikes. Most of the horses were stopped dead in their tracks and thrown over backwards or to one side as they impaled themselves.

Everywhere there were screams and cries and, almost simultaneously, many loud snaps as the weight of an impaled horse or rider broke a pike despite its sturdy thickness.

One horse and rider actually broke through and for a brief moment his swinging broadsword wreaked havoc and casualties among our pike men—until he was brought down by arrows shot at close range, at the same time a strongly swung sword slashed the horse's right front leg so severely that it was almost severed.

The knight's horse knocked over a number of archers as it collapsed with a scream so loud it could be heard above the din.

****** *William*
I may have been the captain of our forces, but my personal part in the battle was quite limited. For a few moments, we all watched the King's knights and men surge out of the gate as if we'd all been struck dumb.

But then my shouts and Henry's shouts for the men to stand to their positions was picked up by the sergeants and then, a few moments later, Peter and Richard and I and all the archers notched our lights and began pushing out arrows at a tremendous pace.

At some point, as the King's knights began their charge and got closer, I remember switching to my heavies and watching the pike men in front of me set the butts of their pikes and kneel as low as possible behind their shields so we could see the approaching attackers and shoot over their heads.

There was much shouting and grunting all around me as the archers launched arrow after arrow from their longbows. Very few of the King's horsemen reached our line and those that did created havoc as they crashed into our pikes and their horses were impaled.

The horses were stopped in their tracks by the pikes, but not all the riders—one of them came flying through the air and knocked me off my feet as he crashed headfirst straight into me and the archers behind me.

In a trice, Peter hauled me to my feet whilst Richard covered me with his shield. As I struggled to my feet and began searching for my bow, I could see one of Albert's archers behind me holding a dagger in both hands as he crouched over the fallen rider's helmeted head and pushed downward with a mighty push into the helmet's eye slit and the man's legs and arms began to jerk about as if he had the shaking pox.

****** *William*

"Stand firm. Push at the enemy foot. Stand firm. Push at the foot soldiers." Henry's new order was quickly taken up by the sergeants.

And that's what we all did. The men running

behind the knights did not have time to reach our lines before our archers began shooting them down and our pike men with broken pikes snatched up their swords and shields and kneeled as they wait for the charge to reach them.

It was the pike men's job to prevent the enemy infantry from reaching the archers. They were kneeling and crouching low behind their shields so the archers standing behind them could shoot over their heads and straight into the approaching enemy. It was something they practised almost every day.

None of the King's foot soldiers even got close enough to our lines to experience our bladed pikes.

Our archers were good shots and instinctively concentrated on the thrusters—many of whom went down with five or six arrows in them. Those still lumbering down the hill increasingly threw their shields away and turned to run. It left their backs unprotected. As you might expect, many of them didn't make it back to the castle gate.

****** *William*

Within the space of just a few minutes, the slope in front of us was littered with hundreds of dead and wounded enemy knights and men-at-arms. Very few of King Guy's men reached the safety of the castle gate before it swung shut and trapped some of them outside. After a minute or so, the gate cracked back open and let the trapped men rush in.

"First line forward to take prisoners. We need

prisoners to exchange for our men in the castle. Take prisoners. Don't kill them."

That was the order from Henry as the King's men still living on the ground in front of us tried to struggle to their feet to escape.

Our first line of pike men moved up the slope with their shields held up as they got within possible range of arrows from the castle. Every so often one of the King's men tried to resist or was approached by one of our pike men who for some reason or another ignored Henry's order. The result was inevitably a final scream and a chopping sound.

****** *William*

It was over. We all leaned on our bows and watched as a few of the King's wounded men staggered up to the gate in the castle's curtain wall and it once again opened to admit them.

"Well done, lads. Well done. That'll learn the bastards."

That's what I keep saying loudly over and over as I lead my little band of assistants and guards out of Albert's company and walked down the open area in front of our lines.

Henry came trotting over to where I was standing, and we stood together and watched as our pike men moved forward to strip the weapons and armour off the dead and wounded men in front of our lines.

"Quick, Henry," I said as I watched a couple of our men finish off a screaming knight. "Get out there and make sure we take some prisoners. We may need them to exchange for Yoram and his men."

Then over the protestations of Peter and Richard, I led my little command group out into the field to look at the King's men and horses. They were strewn everywhere from our front lines all the way up to the gate in the castle's wall.

One knight whose eyes are still flickering must have particularly drawn the archers' attention—arrows were sticking out of him and his horse everywhere. He was in agony and beyond any hope of repair, so I took my dagger and finished him with a soldier's mercy into his left eye.

I couldn't be sure because of his injuries and pain-distorted features, but he may have been one of the Limassol castle knights who sailed with us to Alexandria.

Then I realised I was terribly thirsty even though the sun had not yet come over the hill and begun shining on the field as it passed overhead. And if I'm thirsty, so must everyone else be as well.

"Peter, Richard, run back to the companies and tell their sergeant captains I said to send water parties into the city."

Chapter Twelve

Aftermath of battle.

Captured weapons and clothes were in piles, and our men were sitting in the shade of the wall quietly talking and tending to our wounded when the castle gate opened. Some of the men stood up to look when the old priest came out and once again began walking down the cart path towards us.

This time I stood up but stayed in the shade and didn't walk out to meet him.

"Coming to count us again?" I inquired sweetly when the heavily sweating man reaches me.

"I have good news," he told me as he wiped his brow and gave me an insincere smile. "The King will accept your terms."

"I'm sure he would," I answered with a laugh.

"But now it's much too late for that and you know it. My offer was made yesterday for the purpose of avoiding a battle. Your king rejected it and now some of my men have been killed or wounded—too many of them thanks to their experience and training, and, of course, thanks particularly to the stupidity of your king, but more than enough to change my terms."

Then I laid out my terms as I poked the priest on the chest with my pointing finger each time I named one: "If my men are alive and in good condition and immediately released, I will let the King live and he can hold his throne in return for the heads of everyone involved in the capture of my men—and ten thousand silver coins so that each of the men here with me can be paid five.

"In addition, I want one thousand bezant gold coins for my trouble and expenses, the permanent end of taxation on the city and merchants of Limassol, the ownership of Limassol castle and all the abandoned mines on the island, and the right to take any and all the trees I want from the King's lands."

Then I snarled as I told him the alternative.

"If my men are not immediately released, or if any of my property and men are in any way ever bothered again, or if my terms are not immediately and fully met, I am going to hang the head of every man in the castle on a spike, including yours and the King's—and take everything for myself and my archers."

"But I'm a priest and he's a king!" the priest protested indignantly.

"Right, you are. Yes, of course. Thank you for reminding me. Well, you're right. You're both certainly deserving of some special attention—I'll hang your bodies from the city wall in addition to your heads."

****** *William*

There was much cheering and shouting when the castle gate opened about thirty minutes later and Yoram and his men walked out. Or perhaps staggered out is a better way to put it since some of them seemed dazed and confused. We rushed forward to greet them as the castle gate closed behind them.

"Are you all right, Yoram? What happened?"

"Water. In the name of God, give us water," he croaked.

Yoram's story began to unfold after we got some water into him from one of the archers' water skins. Then, with Henry and me holding his arms so he wouldn't fall, we tried to walk him down the hill to get away from the castle. As we walked, I pressed him for the names of everyone involved. The King's chancellor and the governor of Limassol were high on the list.

We got Yoram about halfway down the hill when his eyes rolled up into the back of his head and his knees buckled. He could go no farther. He wasn't very heavy so a sweating and puffing Richard picked him up and threw him across his shoulders in a wounded man's carry.

With Peter and I each holding one of Richard's elbows to help him keep his balance, Richard carried Yoram down the cart track to join our wounded men in the shade by the city wall. Whilst we were slowly making our way down the cart path to the city gate, a couple of my swordsmen ran ahead to make sure there will be a shady spot and water and wine available for him and the other captives when we get them there.

The other men in Yoram's party were in

somewhat better shape but not by much—and I was seething.

I almost hope the priest didn't tell the King my terms about the heads and coins and concessions I required. I'd told him we would either immediately get the heads of those responsible and the coins and concessions or, no matter how long it took, the King's head was coming off and so was the head of everyone else in the castle. I was starting to hope they would decide to continue fighting.

******

Yoram and our wounded were in the shade of the city wall, being treated by a couple of hurriedly summoned Famagusta barbers and plied with wine and the pain-deadening flower paste, when the priest appeared again two hours later. The castle gate opened and the priest came out followed by a couple of the castle's slaves pulling a cart. Lord Alstain's head was one of the six fresh cut heads stacked on the sacks of coins.

"Count the coins carefully," I ordered Richard and Peter. They looked at me in surprise when, after a brief pause, I added, "Hopefully, there won't be enough."

Of course, I told them to count the coins carefully; I don't trust the bastard.

****** *William*

By the next afternoon, the coins were safely on our galleys, some of our wounded men and prisoners had died, and Yoram and others were as ready to travel as they ever would be. It was time to return to Limassol and return to earning our coins carrying refugees and merchants and taking Moslem galleys.

We left the King's dead on the field for him to tend. And he'd better hurry—it's hot, and they were already beginning to swell up and smell; his wounded we moved into the shade with water. Except for three French knights, most of them were local men; so I gave the barbers a few coins to tend to the poor sods and told them to leave the French knights out in the sun for the King to worry about.

People lined the cobblestoned street and clapped and cheered as we walked through the city to the quay with Yoram and our wounded men and the captured weapons on hastily assembled horse carts and wains.

We were ready to leave as soon as the local priests finished saying the proper words and waving their crosses over our dead. There were only four of them. I gave the priests a few coins so they'd be buried in the cemetery of the old church even though they probably weren't very good Christians and one was almost certainly a heathen.

I doubt the words and where we planted them will do much good, but you never know, do you?

****** *William*

Our trip back to Limassol was relaxed and everyone was in good spirits, despite the rough seas we encountered coming around the north side of the island.

One of our wounded men unexpectedly died, but Yoram and most of our wounded and captured men spend their days resting on the deck in the sunlight and recovering nicely. The "soldier's friend" flower paste and the goodly amount of wine we carried out of Famagusta were quite helpful in bringing them around.

Yoram and Henry and I spent most of the voyage talking. Yoram thinks the King's chancellor, Lord Alstain, was the man responsible for his being captured and held for ransom.

Henry smiled broadly and nodded his confirmation when I informed Yoram that we had no idea where most of Alstain was these days, but we'd recently seen his head on the cart carrying the coins the King paid to save his life and dynasty.

Then we talked and talked about the King's other concessions and how we might use the old mines and the logs and wood from the trees, and how he and Henry were to respond if the King in any way reneged on our peace agreement—immediately gather up your men and take them to Nicosia, or wherever he is, starve him out, and then kill him and every single one of his knights and courtiers. Until then, be nice.

We agreed one of the very first things we should do is send a couple of men to the king's court in Nicosia to act as our spies so we'll always know the King's strength and, thus, the size of the force Yoram and Henry will need to send to defeat him if it becomes necessary.

Henry suggested a most useful idea—we'll use Aaron and some of the King's coins to quietly buy or establish a tavern or alehouse near the castle gate, a place where the King's men can congregate and drink cheap wine. Even better, Henry thinks he has just the man to run it; a good-natured older pike man from Ireland with a recently acquired Cypriot wife. We'll also try to get someone into the castle. *Henry's more than just a good soldier, isn't he? He's a thinker, that's what he is.*

****** *William*

A huge crowd of cheering and waving people were waiting for us as we bumped up against the quay and began to tie up in one of the mooring spaces.

I spotted an anxious and very pregnant Lena standing next to Harold and nudged Yoram to call the two of them to his attention. She was clinging to her infant daughter and obviously desperately searching for Yoram. And, by God, there's Randolph and young Anderson. They must have come in whilst we were in Famagusta.

The look of relief and joy on Lena's face when Yoram got to his feet and she saw him makes me feel very good indeed—and for some reason I began thinking of my son and brother and felt very much alone. I miss them very much and for some reason I suddenly felt my eyes watering and had to turn away to rub them.

Chapter Thirteen
Lessons learnt and my life is changed.

All of the day following our return was spent sitting in the shade with my senior sergeants and sergeant captains having serious talks. What have we learnt from our experiences at Famagusta? What should we do different? That sort of thing.

I haven't told anyone yet but I have decided to start for England in a few days and return next spring with all the archers I can muster. The Moslem pirates are getting stronger, our galleys and cogs are woefully under-crewed with fighting men, and we need a stronger force here on Cyprus to defend our fortress.

One thing came across loud and clear. We need to keep more men here to guard this place and much more food in it, and in our other fortified posts, so we cannot be starved out before a relief force arrives from England.

Another thing we all agreed is facing charging knights with just two lines of pike men in front of three lines of archers is not enough. From now on we must require every fighting man serving on our galleys and cogs to qualify as an archer and be fully trained and equipped to fight together with the very latest modern weapons—a longbow with armour-piercing arrows, one of Brian's bladed pikes, a shield, and a sword.

I damn well know two lines of pike men are not enough. Got knocked down on my arse in the third line, didn't I?

"And a metal helmet, a water skin, and a breastplate," Henry added as he looked up from whittling away on a piece of wood with his dagger.

"I can do it," Brian agreed, "but I'll need more smiths and more iron and more bow wood, and, of course, more space and more fletchers and bow makers."

Yoram made much of the need to strengthen our citadel. He wanted permission to install interior walls and bastions on all our Limassol walls "just like they were starting to build in Damascus before the Saracens took it." He used a stick to scratch an outline in the dirt whilst he explained to us what a bastion is and why we need to install bastions and interior walls to strengthen our defences.

Bastions and compounds with interior walls quartering them are the very newest thing in military thinking and sound quite sensible to me. They'd sure as hell be much harder for an attacker to break into.

In any event, Yoram is probably right about the need to improve our defences. Indeed, after all he's been through, we'd probably agree to just about anything that might strengthen this place and make it safer for everyone. And why not? Our new recruits and refugees can build the bastions and interior walls with our newly acquired wood and stones.

******

Once the building program for the months ahead was settled, our talk turned to recruiting and training and what to do about a local moneylender who apparently cheated some of our men out of their prize money.

To a man, our senior sergeants were concerned that we have too many men who do not speak English well enough to understand their commands or come to them with their problems. And I certainly agree with their concerns and tell them as much.

What I don't mention is Thomas's similar concern that we don't have enough senior sergeants who can read and do sums.

"You're right, of course, and the only place to get the archers we need is England and Wales. That's why I've decided to go back to England early this year—so I'll have time to recruit more archers to bring back with me when I return in the spring."

Besides, I'm getting very homesick to see George and Thomas.

"Actually, I'm thinking about leaving very soon, within the next week or two if possible, because of our new arrangements with the merchants. That will give me time to stop in Beirut and Antioch, and maybe even Constantinople, on my way back to England—the places where we might decide to establish our own offices or even fortified compounds such as this one."

And, of course, I'll be visiting other ports along the way, which I'm not about to mention until we're almost to them.

Thomas, I reminded everyone, is very actively recruiting and training archers at Restormel. He apparently has a hundred or more men ready to send out to join us; maybe even two hundred by now—and almost all of them speak English. Then I told them what I am thinking of doing with the apprentice archers and asked them what they thought of my plan.

"I have a mind to have Thomas immediately send out both them and the most likely of the apprentice archers instead of waiting until next spring and bringing them with me when I return. If they come out now, Henry and his sergeants can spend the winter training them to use Brian's pikes and walk about in step.

"Then they'll be here to help you if the King misbehaves. And if they're already here you'll also be able to start using them on your galleys and cogs next year, as soon as the sailing season starts."

Everyone nodded their heads in agreement, and Yoram looked much relieved. He should be—it means he will soon have several hundred additional archers to help guard his family this winter when I'm not here.

Yoram perked up considerably when he heard the news and began talking about where they might be barracked and how much additional food and firewood he and Thomas Cook will need to buy and where it might be stored if our Cyprus compound is to survive a long siege until relief arrives.

Then we talked about what we might try to do in Constantinople, Antioch, and Beirut, and how we might do it. It gave me a headache just thinking about all the different possibilities.

****** *William*

Getting ready to return to England with stops along the way required me to tie up all kinds of loose ends. One of the first things I did was walk to the market with Peter and Richard to talk again with Aaron, Reuben, and the other merchant leaders. As you might imagine, we had many things to talk about now we've settled the question of where the merchants will be in as our agents and how many escape galleys they will hire.

It's always good to see our new partners, and their welcome was warm and sincere. I finally opened our real conversation when the absolutely required tea and food and the extensive pleasantries of personal health and family inquiries were finished. I did so after three bowls of tea, eating some delicious newly arrived figs, and learning Aaron has a new son and none of us or our families have any serious new poxes.

"Aaron, in a couple of days, these two young men and I are going to take a couple of galleys and make a voyage to visit Beirut and Antioch, and maybe even Constantinople, to inquire about setting up some kind of permanent compounds or offices. Do you have any suggestions for us?"

Aaron certainly did, and so did just about everyone else. We spent hours eating and talking about what the company of archers might do and how we might do it.

We also talked about the merchants' plans for placing agents and hiring escape galleys in the ports along the Holy Land coast; and about where we might be able to find alchemists and coiners and buy the blocks of silver, iron, and copper they would need to produce coins.

Among other things, the merchants agreed to help us find an alchemist who knows how to separate silver, iron, and copper from the rocks they apparently come in. It apparently requires melting the rocks and only alchemists know how to do it.

****** *William*

Our afternoon was coming to a successful conclusion after a long afternoon of talking. I had a much better grasp of things as we stood up and started to leave with smiles all around.

"Oh, please, don't go yet, William, I have a great favour to ask of you," said Reuben from Latika. The other merchants were smiling as he gently but firmly pushed me back on to the pillows where I'd been sitting.

"My brother has a unique problem with a slave. He needs to solve before he moves to Alexandria to represent the archers there, and we all think you're just the man to solve it."

"I don't buy slaves and I don't keep them. I free them, as you know."

"That's it exactly. It is a gift to you because he wants the slave freed and properly cared for and kept by someone such as you, not sold or given away or cast out to starve."

A gift. Damn it. I can't refuse a gift. He'd be insulted.

"Of course I would be honoured to accept your brother's gift. Please thank him for me."

"Oh, thank you, thank you. He'll be pleased and she will be too. She's heard all about you and is very happy to pledge her liege to you."

She? She?

"She?"

"Oh yes. And very well trained in household matters by her mother, isn't she? My brother got her mother off a Frenchman in Beirut some years ago to settle a debt, and she came along soon afterwards.

"My brother thinks she may be his but he isn't sure. That's why he wants her with a good man such as you, because she might be his daughter you understand."

Oh my God.

I was still sitting there trying to understand what just happened when Reuben returned leading a young woman—who promptly prostrated herself in front of me and placed my foot on her head.

What have I done?

"Thank you for freeing me and accepting me as your vassal, Master," the girl said in French after I moved my foot and motioned her to stand up. She said it with her eyes looking down at the ground. Then she darted a look up at me with the bluest eyes I've ever seen.

Bloody hell; where did those eyes come from?

I was literally speechless and all of the merchants and my men were smiling broadly, too damn broadly. *Now what should I do?*

"Er. Oh. Please stand over there until it's time to go. Uh. Are you hungry or thirsty?"

"No, Master. Thank you for asking."

******

I was periodically holding my head in dismay, and my men were all smiling at each other as we walked back to the compound. My new vassal was obediently walking three steps behind me. I truly didn't know whether to laugh or cry or be angry or pleased. But she certainly did have blue eyes.

"Uh. Yoram, when we get back to the compound, would you please ask Lena to show her where the piss pot and shite hole and kitchen are located, and things like that?"

Christ. I don't even know her name.

So I stop and turn around and ask.

"What is your name?"

"Helen, Master."

Chapter Fourteen
The change is delightful

Our arrival back at our little tower created an absolute uproar. Someone, probably Peter, must have run ahead, for when we got there everyone's bedding and personal clothes and weapons was either already gone or being moved out, except mine. And without initially saying a word, but wearing a big smile, Harold began scooping up his.

"I'm off to the cog's cabin, aren't I?" he asked no one in particular as he headed for the door.

Yoram scooted up the stone staircase and a few minutes later down waddled a very pregnant Lena with a big smile and little Aria tucked into her arms. She'd come to show Helen around. I just stood there dumb as a stone.

Finally, I decided it was time to start being useful again, so off I went to talk to Brian and see how his smiths and fletchers were doing. He stood and gave me a very big and knowing smile as I walked up to the wooden shed where the women were working on our new arrows and bows.

"I see you've already heard."

Brian responded by nodding his head. Then he couldn't contain himself and he started roaring with laughter and then, to make matters even more embarrassing, so did all the women sitting on the carpets fletching arrows.

I couldn't control myself either. I started laughing too. And then, to make matters worse, when the laughing finally stopped and Henry and I were talking about the new pikes, the women started giggling and making quiet little comments to each other with periodic nods of their heads towards me.

All I could do was lift both hands in resignation and shrug my shoulders and smile back at them—which caused more peals of laughter and even bigger smiles.

******

The evening started with all the makings of a disaster. Helen ran off to Thomas Cook's kitchen and brought me food and drink. Then she crossed her legs and sat down to watch me eat. It made me nervous. I hadn't eaten alone in years and never with someone just staring at me.

"For God's sake, go get some food and wine for yourself. I don't like eating alone and I don't like people staring at me when I eat."

"Yes, Master."

"And stop calling me 'Master'. You're my pledged vassal now, not a slave. My name is William."

"Yes, Master."

My supper was very nice and the second bowl of wine she ran and fetched for me improved my mood quite a bit. We talked about various things. Helen spoke French because of her mother, and I learnt a lot because I had her tell me all about herself.

Helen didn't know how old she was and she seemed to be quite an innocent. She'd never even been out of her family's compound until her Uncle Reuben came to fetch her and brought her to Cyprus with a woman servant as a chaperone. It was very cold on the galley and they didn't have any blankets. But now, she brightly volunteered, she knows why her mother told her one of her duties would be to sleep with me to keep me warm.

Oh jeezu.

I left the candle burning after I got back from using the shite hole and sat down on the string bed I use to keep me off the cold floor. Helen immediately ran over and knelt down to take off my sandals.

"May I rub your shoulders and massage your body, Master? My mother taught me how. My mother said that when I had a master he would enjoy being massaged and touched. Is it true?"

"Er. Yes, I think so. Yes, I'm sure your mother is right."

What followed surprised me. Yes, it truly did. She promptly ran around behind me, put her hands under my shirt, and began kneading my shoulders. It was quite pleasant and relaxing. It was something new and I liked it, and I told her so.

"Oh good. I was hoping you'd like it. Will you lie down on the bed, Master, so I can massage and touch the rest of you?"

So I did and she does and she was quite thorough about it. Then she really surprised me.

"Oh good. I'm making your little man thing happy. My mother said I'll know it is happy if it gets bigger and you will let it give me a present if I make it really happy by massaging and kissing it."

"A present?"

"Oh yes, Lord. She said if I am a good servant you'll enjoy it when your man thing gives me a present of gravy in my mouth that will taste good or a present of gravy when you put your man thing in the hole between my legs where I piss.

"She says when you put it in me will feel really good for both of us once I get used to it. Is she right, Lord? Will you let me have it if I please you enough? Oh, I hope I can please you so your wife doesn't get it all. I'll try. I really will."

My wife? Oh my God.

"Uh. Umm. Yes. I'm sure your mother is right. Of course, she is. Umm. What else did she tell you?"

Chapter Fifteen
Things are changing.

We've been regularly sending galleys to Beirut to pick up refugees. It's a place I know something about because I'd been there myself years ago with King Richard and more recently when I went with Lord Edmund when he visited the city's Christian quarter to try to recruit more men.

Since I already knew the city, I decided to let someone else go so I could stay in Cyprus for a few more weeks and enjoy my new and very changed life with Helen.

Helen was quite enjoyable despite being a bit strange; she even filled a leather bucket with water and a bowl of white wine and washed me all over. She said it would kill the itchy lice in my hair and around my dingle.

I was quite fearful at first because I'd heard that washing weakens a man. But she was so insistent I decided to risk it. Truth be told, it felt sort of good.

****** *William*

Instead of going myself to look at Beirut as a

possible port to pick up refugees, I sent Randolph with two galleys. They are going with their crews at refugee-carrying levels—so they'll be able to carry as many refugees as possible and still put up a good fight if they are attacked. Whilst he is there, it will be Randolph's job to look for some sort of home or compound we could use if we decide to station a few archers there permanently with someone as our post sergeant.

Besides, I decided, if I stay in Cyprus longer, the galleys going to England with me would be able to make more trips to the Holy Land ports and gather more coins by carrying refugees to safety.

Another reason I decide to stay in Cyprus a bit longer is that I'm still concerned about the King— although, so far, we haven't heard a peep out of him. He's probably busy trying to find replacements for the men whose heads he took to save his own.

In any event, Randolph sailed for Beirut yesterday with two galleys. He was not going to Beirut alone. Richard Kent and Peter Sergeant are with him and so is Andy Anderson, who just returned from Acre where he'd been Simon's chosen man and apparently did quite well.

The three young ones don't know it, or perhaps they did if their enthusiasm about sailing with Randolph was any guide, but Yoram and I had seriously discussed promoting them to senior sergeants and giving them a port and some archers to sergeant. *If only they could scribe and sum.*

Aaron the merchant is also travelling with Randolph. He'll be Randolph's interpreter if one is needed and help introduce him to the local merchants and officials.

Between the five of them, they have more than enough experience to know what we want and what we need. Yoram and I were looking forward to getting their thoughts and suggestions when they return.

Everything we've heard so far suggests Beirut has real prospects for us since the Saracens seem to be heading that way now that they've taken Jerusalem. But how long can Beirut hold out against Saladin and his Kurds, and who should we send there if we decide to proceed?

We weren't only looking at Beirut for a new refugee carrying opportunity, of course. We were also looking at other large ports without refugees—because Yoram thought there might be a lot of refugees and merchants willing to pay handsomely to get themselves safely to those ports instead of Limassol. Indeed, making it possible for refugees and merchants to pay to safely get to ports other than here on Cyprus was the main reason we were considering opening up posts elsewhere.

The other reason for opening new posts, of course, was to earn coins carrying foolish Christians, such as crusaders and pilgrims, *to* the Holy Land when our galleys return to pick up more refugees. The pilgrims and crusaders who might be willing to pay us to carry them would be, of course, either blissfully ignorant as to the reception they'll receive from the Saracens when they try to get to Jerusalem or have serious death wishes. But they also have coins, and who am I not to help them get to wherever it is they want to go?

Randolph and his men returned from their trip to
Beirut with a lot of information and two galleys full of
refugees and coins. He and the sergeants I sent with him
all agree we should try to establish a refugee evacuation
post near the great Beirut quay. They also recommended
we greatly increase our galley visits to Beirut because of
the increasing flow of refugees trickling out of Damascus
and the Christian manors around it.

Aaron stayed in Beirut. Randolph brought me a
parchment from him saying he'd talked to the local
merchants and clergy and thinks we might be able to
profitably station two or three escape galleys here for
them to use to escape in when the Saracens come. Some
of the local fishermen, he said, are making similar offers
but are not trusted the way we are. We have, it seems, a
good reputation for fighting off pirates and doing what
we say we will do.

Aaron's decision to stay in Beirut for a while was
something he and I had discussed and negotiated before
he sailed with Randolph. I authorised him to commit up
to four escape galleys to permanently standby to carry the
local merchants and worthies to safety.

Our price for each minimally crewed escape
galley standing by for one year will be the same as we are
charging in Acre and Alexandria. Aaron and his agents
will keep one in every ten of the escape galley coins they
collect from the local merchants and other worthies—and

they are for emergency evacuations only; they cannot use them to carry paying passengers and cargos.

****** William

It's time for me to take a look at Constantinople and Antioch now that Randolph and his men have returned from Beirut. I can't put it off any longer. And after I do, I'll head on to England via Malta and the coasts of Spain and France. Helen is going with me to England and so are a number of our men and galleys.

Not every man and galley going with me to England will be sailing there via Constantinople. Our galleys are earning too many coins hauling refugees to justify moving them away from the Holy Land until absolutely the last minute.

The large amount of coins we are earning is why I am only planning to take Randolph and my two fetchers and helpers, Peter and Richard, and three of our sturdiest galleys to Antioch and Constantinople; we'll rendezvous with the rest of our England-bound galleys and men in Malta in six weeks—and then, although our men and pilots don't know it yet, we're going travel a route we haven't travelled before.

And, yes, Helen is coming with me; I want her to see England.

Harold won't be captaining my galley this time. Instead, he'll be organising and leading the ten or eleven galleys of ours which will be sailing from Cyprus straight to our rendezvous in Malta—and each of them will be carrying a chest of coins.

Harold's good at organising such things, isn't he?

We'd take more galleys and coin chests to England but we are so short of archers Harold's galley may not be able to each carry more than ten. We are limited as to how many archers can return to England with our coins because we have to leave enough men behind to guard our compound and man the galleys that will stay behind to continue carrying refugees from the Holy Land ports.

Recruiting more men from England and Wales to become apprentice archers is vital if we are to continue growing the chests of coins we'll need for George's future, at least, that's what Thomas says.

Six weeks should be more than enough time for me to check out Antioch and Constantinople and then get to Malta in time to rendezvous with Harold's fleet. Randolph, Bob Farmer, and Angelo, and will sail with me and so will Peter Sergeant and Richard Kent. Henry will stay behind to continue training our new recruits and command our men in the event of an attack.

One of the three galleys I'm taking, mine because it will be going all the way to England, will carry two chests of coins secreted in its ballast—a king's ransom in each chest so to speak. Each of the galleys sailing with Harold will also carry one of the coin chests and as many paying passengers as we can cram on board. Evan will be the sergeant captain of my galley.

Hopefully, our men won't know about the chests and the pirates won't find out about them. Our men are

good lads but being so near to so many coins might tempt
them too much, eh?

Randolph's and Bob Farmer's galleys will carry
no coins since they will be returning to Cyprus or to
wherever Randolph and Bob end up being stationed as
the post sergeants. Where they will be is something we'll
decide whilst we're in Constantinople.

Some of our cogs may also sail to Malta with
Harold's galleys as escorts and perhaps on to England;
but, of course, they'll only join us on our voyage to
England if they have sufficient cargos and paying
passengers.

Yoram thinks every galley and cog we decide to
send will be oversubscribed. He says the initial response
from the refugees on Cyprus has been tremendous. Some
are offering tremendous sums to be carried all the way to
France and England and all those who want to return to
Europe see getting to Malta as being a major step towards
getting further away from danger and closer to their
homes.

******

Everything has changed. Randolph just told me
that he really likes Beirut and would like to be the senior
sergeant in charge of our men and galleys if we set up a
post and escape galleys there.

"It's much nicer than Alexandria, William, and
I've been thinking of changing my mind about going
back to England with you. I mean, there's nobody back
there for me, is there?"

I'd never mentioned to Randolph my real reason for bringing him back from Alexandria—to be our senior sergeant in Constantinople if it turns out we need one there as I expect. He's always been our most dependable archer, hasn't he?

"Well, you did splendidly in Alexandria and you're certainly the man most qualified to set us up in a new port. That's for sure. But I've heard good things about Constantinople too. Much better things, actually."

Then I explained to Randolph what I meant.

"If I've heard right, it's bigger and there's less fighting amongst the local people these days—that sort of thing."

And then we both laughed when I teased him by pointing to the luxurious and well-barbered beard, which is his pride and joy.

"Besides, you'll be safe even if Constantinople falls to the Saracens—because, with that beard, they're not likely to recognise you as the Christian pirate you are." It was a joke I'd made and we both roared: the Christian knights and their men have begun shaving their beards, probably because the Moslems don't and it proves their blades are sharp.

What isn't a joke is the crusaders who think anyone wearing a beard is a Moslem and kill him out of hand—and it is the crusaders who everyone says are coming to take Constantinople, not the Saracens.

"Aye, I've heard the same. But I've seen Beirut and I like it. It's a bird in the hand, so to speak."

"Aye. You're right about that, and if it's Beirut

you want to sergeant, you shall certainly have it. But, by God, I've a thought. How about sailing with me next week when I go to look at the opportunities for us in Antioch and Constantinople? You could help me check them out and then go be the senior sergeant in Beirut or wherever you choose."

Chapter Sixteen
The long way home.

Three galleys rowed out of Limassol two mornings later. I was in the big one with Evan as its sergeant captain and a crew of seven sailors and eighty-eight archers—one for each oar. Richard, Peter, and Aaron are with me and so, of course, is Helen. I've got the little captain's castle and she and Lena fixed it up quite comfy with our own bedding and piss pot; Evan and the other sergeants are sharing the bigger castle in the stern of the galley.

I was not the only one who watched with a great deal of amusement and pleasure as Helen walked with a look of determination on her face down to the quay where the galley was moored—leading one of Henry's donkey carts with an equally serious-looking Lena and a great pile of bedding and pots and clothes piled on it. The women were obviously determined not to be denied and no one was brave enough to try stop them, certainly not me.

Randolph and Bob Farmer were each in command of one of the other two galleys. Their galleys were only slightly smaller with four fewer oars on each side. They too were sailing with a full crew of seven sailors and eighty archers. Only my galley was carrying coin chests instead of rocks in some of its ballast space.

In addition to its regular sailors, each of our galleys is carrying enough additional sailors for two prize crews; one for a cog, the other for a galley. They'll help with the rowing and sailing of the galleys until we take some prizes—and that probably won't be until after we leave Malta. *But you never know, do you?*

We rowed out through the returning Limassol fishing fleet with many a wave and good cheer. There was a time early on when the local fishermen viewed us as possible slavers to be avoided the way they avoided the Islamic pirates who used to raid hereabouts before we arrived. Those days are long gone; today we're valued customers for all the fish we buy for Friday's meals and a number of the local fishermen and their sons have signed on to join us as sailors and archer trainees.

******

The weather was good, and we rowed into Antioch's harbour five days later—and even though there were only three galleys we caused quite a scare. It seems word had just reached the city that King Leo of Armenia is marching on Antioch with an army that includes the Knight Hospitallers.

It seems there are conflicting claims to the city because the count who had been its previous overlord, a vassal of King Leo, died without an heir—fighting at Hattin for King Guy of Jerusalem, the very same King Guy who, as the new King of Cyprus, just tried to hold

Yoram for ransom.

As the local merchants told us, with much emotion and waving of hands, there is going to be a war because they and the rest of the city's residents prefer a distant relative of their late ruler and refuse to acknowledge Leo's right to name another of the late count's distant relatives as their new ruler.

Whatever its cause, the coming war over Antioch is a fine opportunity for us. We no more than tied up at the quay then we were besieged with people wanting to escape the city and the coming fighting—Orthodox Christians who want to escape to Constantinople; Roman Catholic Christians who want to escape to Cyprus or any place where the Roman religion is practised; and Jews who want to go anywhere they will be safe. Even better, it seems everyone with a hoard of coins wants to send some of them to safety so they won't be destitute and starve if they are forced to flee.

****** *William*

There was no time to lose. I stripped Bob's and Randolph's galleys of all but the minimum number of sailors and archers they would need to carry refugees and we began collecting coins, lots of coins, from those who were willing to pay to flee to Cyprus. Both galleys would go back to Cyprus under new sergeant captains so Bob and Randolph can remain here with me. Their passengers will do most of the rowing.

I quickly wrote two parchments to Yoram describing the situation. He was to immediately start sending our galleys and cogs to Antioch as fast as they became available. One parchment would go on each galley to make sure my message get through to Yoram.

Bob Farmer would remain to be our man in Antioch with Peter Sergeant or one of the other archer sergeants as his deputy. Because the situation was so dangerous, Bob and Peter would always keep one galley in port until the next galley arrives. And because I was greedy for more coins and saw an opportunity, I offered standby evacuation galleys to the local merchants and priests for double the number of coins we were fetching in Alexandria. They made their marks and paid their coins for four of them for a year.

******

Our galleys begin arriving from Cyprus eleven days later. They were eleven very nice days, and it wouldn't have bothered me if it had taken the galleys even longer to get here. It gave my men and me an opportunity to meet all the local worthies, and for Helen and me, a chance to see the city and visit its market, albeit with a substantial guard of swordsmen and archers in tow. At Helen's insistence, I bought a shite pot so we would not have to get up at night to hang our arses over the side.

Helen is enchanting and I love her dearly.

We even recruited a couple of archers and some soldiers who deserted from the local garrison. They don't know how to use longbows but they've got strong arms and were willing to learn. They'll go to Cyprus on one of the refugee galleys for Henry to learn them to put their feet down at the same time and use longbows and pikes.

At least, I think they're deserters; they certainly scurried into Bob's galley and out of sight fast enough.

All good things must end, and our delightful visit to Antioch was one of them. Randolph kept his galley and all its men and took over as our senior sergeant—and after thirteen days in Antioch, our two remaining galleys began rowing for Constantinople. We carried as many refugees to Constantinople as we could jam into our galleys, in addition to all of our men and another chest of coins. Evan's galley was literally stuffed with seasick refugees and so was Ralph's.

Chapter Seventeen

Constantinople surprises me.

Constantinople was immense. It had, to my great
surprise, fast moving ocean waters flowing past it like
rivers. It was like trying to row up a river to get to the
various city quays. And the fast moving water certainly
must bring a lot fish—there were people all along the
shore fishing and men in little fishing boats casting nets
right up against the shoreline.

It was a fascinating and impressive city with all
its palaces along the waterfront and its great huge church.
I was impressed and so was Helen. Her eyes were wide
with amazement. She never, she told me, ever expected
to see such a sight. Neither did I.

****** *William*

Bringing Orthodox Church believers to safety,
including a large number of priests and bishops who
suddenly needed to leave the doomed city to pursue
religious matters, got us an approval to tie up to the quay
next to the city wall at one of Constantinople's many
harbours, the one nearest the big church.

And, of course, the Orthodox priests and bishops were not the only ones running for safety—an equally large number of priests and bishops of Rome paid equally handsome amounts to get out of Antioch on the galleys we were sending to Cyprus and Beirut.

Either way they travelled, the churchmen all paid the exorbitant number of coins we required—after arguing that they should go free or at reduced rates because they are hurrying off to "do God's work."

We didn't argue about whether abandoning one's flock of believers and running away was God's work; we just held out our hands and took their coins, counted them particularly carefully if they are coming from bishops, and bowed them aboard—but only after each and every one of them assured us they understood they'd be helping with the rowing and immediately thrown overboard if they didn't.

Doing what you don't want to do enriches your soul; isn't that what the good book says?

******

I knew a little about Constantinople when we arrived because one of the Greek priests we were carrying sought me out during the trip and wanted to talk. What he probably really wanted was to get away from having to row. His name was Father Kostas.

"I heard someone in Antioch say you English are not like the other Latins. You don't take slaves and you keep your word. Is it true?"

Latins?

"Latins? What do you mean?"

"Latins, of course; the crusaders, people like you; the men whose priests speak Latin to each other and are coming to here to attack us because we don't bow to your pope and we make a different sign of the cross."

"Nonsense. I'm afraid you've got it wrong. Religion is just an excuse. The crusaders don't care how you worship—they see you're rich and want to steal your treasures and sell you as slaves. Religion is just an excuse."

"Just an excuse? Can it be true?"

Father Kostas seems almost disappointed it won't be a religious war; I wonder why?

"Of course, it's true. I've known many crusaders personally. Hundreds of them, for sure. Maybe thousands. And every one of them was on his crusade for the land and treasure he could get, including me and all my men. Hell, I was once a crusader myself—came out with that lying bastard King Richard myself, didn't I?"

"Really? And you don't like Richard? You surprise me. I thought all the crusaders liked him."

"Only those who don't know the murdering bastard."

****** *William*

The priest told me his name—Kostas something or other, which tangled my tongue so I couldn't say it. But no matter; what I learn from Kostas is interesting. He claims Constantinople is the centre of a great empire with its own pope and a great emperor ruling over many kings.

It all started to go wrong years ago, according to Father Kostas, when some of the emperors began selling concessions to the Venetians and other Latins to carry the empire's cargos and passengers to the rest of the world. It worked for a while, but then the Latins brought in more and more of their families and started their own churches and fighting wars with other Christians for control of the city's markets. Real wars, for God's sake. Inside the city walls.

In the end, the Latins, and particularly the Venetians, fought so much and stole so much and sold too many poxed slaves to the church. As a result, the local pope, or whatever he's called, got seriously pissed and told the people to slaughter all the Latins. That was about twenty years ago.

According to Kostas, killing most of the Venetians and other Latins and selling the rest to the Turks for slaves solved the problem, but only for a while. Orthodox-owned sailing vessels and financing didn't arrive to replace those which were lost—so now the Venetian galleys and merchants and moneylenders are back with new concessions along with some Pisans and Genoese.

This is once again causing troubles with the local people and the Orthodox Church—except this time, the crusaders are coming to help the Venetians keep their concessions.

Help the Venetians, my arse. They're coming to loot and take over.

****** *William*

The priest disappeared as soon as we reached the quay. And so did Aaron. In fact, I think I saw them walking off together towards the nearest gate in the city's huge walls.

Aaron returned a couple of hours later with two men wearing great huge turbans. Aaron introduced them as the leaders of the local merchants and they wanted to talk business, serious business. So we did—and the result was quite interesting.

We'd no more than begun exchanging pleasantries with the merchants, when in rapid succession Father Kostas arrived with a white-bearded, old priest with a long name and title I couldn't get my tongue around, and a couple of messengers arrived from the Emperor's palace.

Father Kosta's elderly companion was obviously a high ranking church official if Kosta's deference to him was any guide; the gaudily dressed palace official, on the other hand, was some kind of court functionary who was visibly distressed when it became apparent I neither recognised his importance nor could understand a word of whatever version of Greek he was speaking.

It was an amazing scene of confusion as Randolph and I stood on the quay with the men who'd come to welcome us. Helen and a number of our men were standing on the galley deck immediately behind us and watching intently.

And I ordered the bows of our men strung just in

case.

Each of the dignitaries wore a great high turban and wanted to speak with me privately but couldn't because we speak different languages. As a result, we all stood there on the quay and everyone interpreted for everyone else—and usually at the same time.

It was so preposterous and chaotic I would have laughed until my sides hurt if I hadn't been so deeply involved. Thomas would have been delighted.

Over time it became somewhat clear—they all want the same thing. Each wants his leader and his leader's high ranking followers to be rescued at the last minute if the crusaders attack; but only if the crusader attack looks like it is going to be successful. Each of the men on the quay, of course, will accompany his leader to safety when he runs. Money, it seems, was no object.

Alright.

Finally, I raised both my hands and bellowed to get everyone's attention. Then one at a time I took each of the men to the side along with Aaron and Father Kostas and gave them a time to meet me here tomorrow so we can discuss matters privately.

"Whatever you desire can be done, but it will require many bezant gold coins in advance. When you return, please bring an interpreter you trust who can speak Latin or French. We will meet in private on the deck of the galley behind me so no one can overhear us. When we meet, you can tell me how many people my galleys will have to carry to safety and where you want my galleys to take them. Then I'll tell you how many gold bezants you will have to pay to get there safely."

******

After the various groups of men left, I send Aaron and Richard Kent to the city's great market to buy maps of the city and the surrounding waters.

"Buy as many different maps as you can buy. Particularly those of the city which show the city gates and those which show the harbours and moorages on the islands and coastline near the city."

It's been a stressful day. I need a glass of wine, a good back rub, and a massage. I hope it's still light enough to see when Aaron and Richard get back with the maps.

But then something important popped into my mind and I called after Aaron and Richard.

We could end up fighting the Venetians if we try to do business here. I wonder how they arm themselves and fight their galleys? Do they use slaves as rowers or fighting men?

"Oh, and one more thing. Whilst you're talking to the mapmakers, try to find out if the Venetians use slaves to row their galleys and how the men on their galleys are armed?"

******

All the next morning whilst we waited for the Emperor's men, Randolph and I studied the maps and discussed how the crusaders might attack the city and how the Venetian galleys might support them if they do.

One thing is for sure. Because of the Venetians and their galleys, we'll need to do things differently and more carefully if we base some of our galleys and men here.

A party of four grandly clothed courtiers arrived three hours late the next day on ornate, slave-carried litter chairs. They were, of course, deliberately late to show us how important they are. It's the custom here as I had been informed and I was suitably impressed. Their turbans were beautiful.

The Emperor's courtiers were the very first of the three groups of potential refugees we will meet today. And there's no surprise in that—the Emperor's involvement means we'll enjoy his permission for everything we agree to do. An hour later, we knew exactly what the Emperor wants. In a nutshell, the Emperor and his court want enough escape galleys standing by to carry three hundred people up the coast to safety whenever the Emperor decides to run.

Aaron tells me the slave-carried litter chairs are called sedan chairs. He doesn't know what the name means. I never did find out.

Normally, three hundred refugees would require two galleys with the refugees doing much of the rowing whilst our archers stand by to do any fighting that might be necessary.

Rescuing the Emperor and his court will be different—all of them will be high dignitaries and their families and retainers, and thus, in general, quite soft and useless. It would be folly to expect any of them to be capable of rowing or fighting. It means we'll need to provide a lot more men and have less room for refugees on each galley.

Hmm. Maybe some of the extra men we supply could simply be strong rowers instead of our highly trained archers.

After the ritual pleasantries were completed and I'd listened to the Emperor's men tell us where they would want to be carried and consulted our maps, I told them it sounded as though they will need five of our war galleys and the price for each for one year would be three thousand bezant gold coins in advance for each galley and a crew of one hundred experienced men.

Also, and this was very important I told the Emperor's men, we required a proper moorage on a very safe quay where our galleys and men can wait for them— such as the one I could see in the distance to my right.

Being from the east as they were, the courtiers took my price of three thousand bezant gold coins as my opening position for our negotiations. An hour later and after much shouting and hand waving and head shaking, they had beaten me down to two thousand gold bezants. They will, of course, tell the Emperor we are being paid a much higher price and keep the difference for their trouble.

All is well because two thousand gold coins was the price I'd had in mind when the negotiations began. But traditions must be observed and we'll undoubtedly go through the same process with the merchants and priests. The gold coins we will receive are called bezants and are struck by the Emperor's coiners.

Of course, we'll take their bezants; they are known and accepted everywhere in the civilised world. Thomas and Yoram will rub their hands with glee when they see them.

Most significantly, we also reached agreement as to where our galleys and men will be based—the next quay over from where we are presently moored. The quay is in front of a long and very narrow stretch of land between the ocean and the high and formidable city wall running alongside it.

The distance between the ocean water and the city wall is so narrow, about one hundred paces where our moorage is located, someone standing on the city wall towering above our camp's site might be able to throw a rock over our camp and the quay into the sea. The city wall had been built such a short distance from the sea so the sea could act as a moat. It's an ideal location for us and it will be where our galleys are moored and our men will live and train.

The city is on a narrow peninsula jutting out into the sea with water on three sides. Aaron says the fourth side, the land side, is protected by great walls and towers. It's the most formidable and strongest position I've ever seen.

Moreover, the courtiers agreed our men could immediately put a new and extremely defensible gate through the city wall, one so narrow and low only one man can get through it at a time and he will have to crouch to do so; it will be the gate our men use to enter the city and the dignitaries and our other passengers use to get to our galleys when they flee.

Our proposed location was instantly accepted by the Emperor's men as soon as they understood the reason we wanted it. They liked the proposed location because the city wall towering over our camp will give them a degree of control over us and insure the safety of their escape galleys; we liked it because it was right next to the water so we could quickly get away. We also like it because we can quickly wall off each end of the narrow strip of land which is our new concession.

Walling off our narrow strip of land is important because it will make it virtually impossible for the crusaders or anyone else to launch a surprise land attack against us, except from the city wall towering above us— and we'll be long gone before the crusaders can fight their way into the city and climb up to the top of the wall to begin throwing things down on us.

At least, I hope we'll be gone in time.

****** *William*

Father Kostas and a gaggle of priests arrived a few hours after the Emperor's courtiers departed. Most were walking quite piously with only one of their elderly, white-haired archbishops riding in a slave-carried chair in front of them. They too were fashionably late to show us their importance, but only by a couple of hours.

Our negotiations were over quickly after the obligatory pleasantries and prayers. The priests obviously knew about the two thousand gold bezants the Emperor is paying for each galley, and we were able to quickly reach an agreement on a similar price. It only took twenty minutes.

The Church wants to charter three galleys because of the importance of "saving both the Patriarch and the extremely important hand of Saint John." Unlike the Emperor and his courtiers, their priests will agree to row. Rowing is apparently unseemly only if one is a bishop or above. The willingness of the priests to row is important; it means we will need fewer men for the galleys chartered by the Church.

Whilst we were waiting for the merchants to arrive, Aaron explained about Saint John's hand. It seems the big church in the city had somehow obtained Saint John the Baptist's hand and encased it in gold. It cures various poxes and problems if one pays the required fee to kiss it and prays correctly.

A couple of hours and a brief nap on the deck in the sun and the merchants arrived. They too already knew about the price we are charging per galley and were willing to pay it. They want to contract for four of our galleys with two hundred refugee places in each galley. Aaron confided their plans to us—they are going to sell some of the seats to pay for their escape and their clients will be required to do the rowing.

"We think your fearsome reputation means we'll need fewer of your sailors and archers to protect each of the galleys. It is a very good thing because it will give us more seats to sell."

The payment terms were the same as those for the Church and the Emperor—half of the coins now and the other half as soon as your specific galleys and men arrive. My plan is to sail for Malta and on to England as soon as the promised evacuation galleys arrive and the payments are safely stored away in Evan's galley for me to carry to England.

******

"Will you do it for sixty gold bezants for one year with young Richard Kent as your sergeant? He can scribe and do sums, you know."

I offered Randolph a great fortune to stay in Constantinople as its senior sergeant. He was stunned and rightly so. Finally, he just nodded.

It's little wonder Randolph was surprised and agreeable—that's ten times more than he earned in Alexandria and more than enough to buy a very nice home and many acres of land anywhere in England, maybe even a title if John is still selling them. No archer has ever been paid so much in his entire life.

"Well then, we better send Evan's galley to Yoram with a parchment telling him to send eleven more galleys here and the type of men we'll need to crew each of them. Eleven is one more than you'll need—and, of course, you'll keep yours here all the time in case you need to make a run for it."

Chapter Eighteen
Domestic bliss.

The next two weeks were among the best of my life. Helen and I moved into the upstairs room of an old wooden merchant's house with a guard detail drawn from the galleys downstairs. It was just inside the wall near where we'd dug through to open the new gate. Every day we would go out to walk in the great city, drink tea in its tea shops, and luxuriate in the warm water of the best public baths. And, of course, we visit the grand bazaar and went shopping almost every day.

Constantinople's grand bazaar was surely one of the world's great wonders with its more than a thousand merchant shops and stalls selling everything imaginable. We bought all kinds of things to take to England—leather rain cloaks, rugs, string beds, chamber pots, cooking spices, candles, lotions, combs, garlic cloves guaranteed to prevent the pox, a mirror, and all kinds of other useless things an astounded Helen suddenly saw as things we absolutely had to have.

Helen was a sight to behold as she went wide-eyed from stall to stall. Even our guards were smiling and pleased at her enthusiasm. She had captured them entirely and our little captain's castle in the front of the galley was soon filled to overflowing.

In one sense, we didn't need the sword- and shield-carrying archers who accompanied us everywhere as our guards. The word was out about our being under the protection of the Emperor, the Church, and the merchants. We were undoubtedly heavily protected— and would have been perfectly safe except for the inconvenient fact the city was boiling with tension and there were armed and anxious Venetians and other potential enemies everywhere in the streets.

I wore my chain mail shirt and carried a sword and my wrist knives at all times. I'm not sure Helen realised the danger and I certainly didn't tell her.

******

Two weeks later, the tenth evacuation galley arrived and everyone promptly paid in full, not that it didn't require a bit of prodding, mind you. But they did and it was time to leave for Malta and England.

What was good, indeed, was who was commanding the tenth galley—Harold, by God. I'd know that red hair and the way he stands anywhere. We waved enthusiastically to each other as his men prepare to throw their mooring lines and some of our men trot down the shore to catch them and pull his galley to a stop despite the moving current.

"Hello, you old fart," I shouted as he jumped over the rail with a big smile and we pounded each other's shoulders. "I'm surprised to see you."

"Well, I got all the galleys off to where they should be and there was nothing more for me to do—so I decided to send Angelo to Malta in my place and come and see for myself what devilment you've got us into this time."

Randolph and I spent most of the day hearing Harold's news and telling him stories about what was happening and showing him around our camp and the city. And we drank more than a few bowls of wine to keep our throats wet whilst we talked. We had a grand old time for two archers and a galley slave who were poor as church mice a few years ago.

Late in the evening, after Helen made one last visit to the market, we boarded Harold's galley and rowed out of the harbour with two archers at every oar and six prize crews to spell them. We rowed away from the quay in the moonlight with a king's ransom of gold coins under the lower rowing benches as part of our ballast.

The crusaders may take Constantinople but, by God, they won't get all its gold.

******

Randolph and many of our captain sergeants were on the moonlit quay as we left in the middle of the night. Our men had long ago broken through the city wall, and the barriers sealing off each end of our concession were mostly up. We're rich and we're suddenly very short of the one thing we thought we had in excess—galleys to send from Cyprus to the Holy Land ports. Randolph had already asked Yoram to send every available galley to help carry the refugees who wanted to leave immediately.

Our big problem at the moment is very big indeed—everyone in the city knows we are leaving and will almost certainly be taking a huge amount of gold coins with us.

I thought about going back to Cyprus to deposit them for safekeeping before heading to Malta. But then I decided against it—it might attract the pirates or even the King to attack Yoram's compound and the men we've left behind.

But my sergeants and I are not exactly virgins in terms of dealing with pirates and robbers, are we? Of course not, we rowed out of our moorage in the middle of the night and we didn't take the best route through the Turkish and Greek islands, or even the second or third best routes. We sailed and rowed far out of our way in the wrong direction before we turned and headed for Malta.

I may be a bit slow sometimes but I'm not stupid.

Chapter Nineteen
Danger along the way.

Our voyage to Malta was different from what other galleys might have done. We were sailing with a very large crew of the best fighting men in the world. And perhaps even more importantly, in terms of getting through to Malta, we'd loaded a cargo primarily of water and bales of arrows and we were going to sail down the middle of the Mediterranean instead of following the coast. We'd be hard to find if anyone was interested in trying to separate us from our coins—and even harder to catch and take if they tried.

****** *William*

      All went well until we had Malta in sight. It was the peak of the sailing season, and we saw various sails coming and going in all directions. Mostly, they turned away and ran when they saw our galley approaching.

      Sighting Malta and seeing a fleet of waiting galleys happened at virtually the same moment.

"Land ahead; land ahead," comes the cry from the lookout on our mast. Almost immediately comes another shout. "Sails to the north; galleys they be."

A few minutes later and the lookout's cry was more ominous. The galleys have turned towards us and there were a dozen or more. Pirates for sure and they've got more of the wind than we do. Worse, the pilots for our galley and the prize crews are on deck and are in agreement—Valletta is to the north where our potential enemies are waiting. We'll have to fight our way through.

Or will we?

Harold and I climbed the mast to see for ourselves. It's true; there they were. So I heaved a big sigh and started down.

"Harold," I shouted whilst I was still climbing down, "it's time to do another wounded bird."

He laughed when I told him the plan.

******

Within minutes we had turned south with our sail up and were running before the wind with the pirates in hot pursuit. Our archers were resting at their oars and talking cheerfully among themselves. Some were napping.

One reason the men were so cheerful is because Harold and I had gone down to the rowing decks and explained my plan to them. To a man, they like it. And they should—they're almost all veterans and saw no reason to risk their lives if it could be avoided by a bit of rowing and a few more hours at sea.

My plan was simple. We'd head south and go the long way all around the island until we come to Valletta and rendezvous with our Cyprus galleys. Of course, if the pirates figured out what we are doing in time, they'd just turn around and go back to Valletta and wait for us to show up there. So we were going to try to entice them to follow us by pretending to flee with the wind behind us—and so far it seems to be working.

We were only showing and using oars from our lower rowing benches, and within an hour, the first of the pursuing galleys began to slowly close on us. The way we were rowing and behaving looked normal to them—it was how a Moorish galley loaded with archers would row because they use galley slaves to do their lower deck rowing. Their sailors and fighting men save their strength and don't row unless it's a dire emergency.

Harold's strongest archers were on deck with their "lights" ready to be launched. "Lights," of course, are a longbow archer's arrows for maximum distance as opposed to their "heavies," which can punch through knights' armour but don't fly as far because of their greater weight.

Our rowing pace picked up more and more as the closest pirate got closer and closer. Although its captain didn't know it, he was already well within range of our longbows and slowly closing the gap. The other pirates were getting closer as well, and we are still not using our upper bank of oars as would be the case if we were short of rowers and long on archers.

Then we tried to appear desperate by having our archers simultaneously launch a huge cloud of arrows. This was exactly the response the pirates would expect from a galley desperately trying to get away and filled with archers.

It worked; our closest pursuer dropped back out of arrow range and we stopped launching them. The others came up but also stayed back just beyond what they thought was our archers' range. Then they all together surged forward and once again came within the distant reach of our archers. And once again we launched a steady stream of arrows until they pulled back.

Hmm. They know we have archers and, yet, they are all coming forward to become targets; is this a pre-arranged effort to share the pain so no pirate galley takes undue punishment until we run out of arrows and they can board us? That's what I'd do—if I didn't know the galley I was after was so strongly crewed or had so many bales of arrows on board.

******

We were leading the unknown galleys further and further away from being able to turn back and go around the island the other way to beat us to Valletta. After three or four hours, they took turns moving up on us once again and we launched a heavy barrage of arrows at each pirate galley as it did.

Once again our pursuers fall back. Before they fell, archers on several of the closer galleys began launching a few of their own arrows at us.

One of their arrows hit home and an archer not ten feet from me went down with an arrow in his leg. Then another was hit in the chest and killed on the spot.

I'm glad I'm wearing my chain link shirt.

"Is it time to turn for Valletta?" I shouted to Harold.

He nodded and I nodded back. Orders were shouted and for the first time the oars on our upper rowing deck were unshipped and began to be used. With two strong men at every oar, we quickly begin to pull away from our exhausted and bloodied pursuers. In less than an hour they disappeared behind us.

******

There were no pirates behind us when night fell and none in sight when we approached the Valletta harbour the next morning. Even so, we were on high alert as we rowed into the harbour—because we didn't know what we might find.

Our concerns were unfounded. What we find, as Harold had earlier assured me we would, is almost all of our England-bound galleys from Cyprus. Only one had not yet arrived.

Cheering and waving erupted from the decks of our anchored and moored galleys as we rowed to the Valletta quay and tied up next to a couple of fishing boats unloading their catches. The various captains and senior sergeants quickly gathered and, of course, old Brindisi hurried down to the quay to get the latest news.

There is nothing Harold and I could do but shake

a lot of hands, clap a lot of shoulders, and repair to the nearby tavern with all the sergeant captains to share our news and get theirs. They all either know or have heard I've got a woman with me, and I got more than a few winks and nudges and inquiries as to whether they can do the same—some quite serious, I think.

Harold and I didn't share everything, of course; certainly not about all the gold bezants we are carrying or our plans for the galleys after we leave Malta.

Even so, the old pirate Brindisi knew about our gold coins and he told me as much as soon as he could walk with me to the alley for a piss and a private word.

"Everyone knows about the gold coins you're carrying, my friend. Even my old captains asked me for permission to go after them. It's probably why you are missing a galley."

"When did they find out?"

He knows; there's no sense denying it.

"Two days ago, after your galleys from Cyprus arrived. An entire fleet of Venetian galleys came in straight from Constantinople and made inquiries. They only stayed for a couple of hours whilst they were taking on water and asking around." *Venetians? Not Moorish pirates?*

"Fortunately, it was after most of your galleys came in or you would probably have lost more than one. But you better take on supplies and leave before the local boys decide to have a go at you whilst you're here. And I certainly don't want the goddamn Venetians or anyone else in these waters taking galleys because they hope it might be your gold galley. I've got a couple of galleys myself, you know, and I don't want to lose them because some stupid Venetian thinks they might be yours."

"Who took my galley? What have you heard?"

"Well, someone probably took it. All I know is that it wasn't my boys because they've been in the harbour all week. Probably the Venetians, I would think."

I took the old pirate's advice and we left for England late that very night. Helen didn't even have a chance to do much more than set foot on the ground and make a brief visit to the market.

What Harold and I did not do is share our plans with our captains until late that afternoon when we were at anchor in the middle of the harbour and getting ready to leave.

******

"Our plan is simple," I told the sergeant captains when they finished assembling on the deck of Harold's galley. "We're going to rendezvous at the mouth of the Alarcon for water. From there, we'll try to take some cogs and galleys from one of the Moslem ports. The prize money will be the same as was for Algiers and payable when we get back to Cyprus."

The sergeant captains, of course, wanted to know which port; Harold and I, of course, told them they'd have to wait to find out.

"No one is to go ashore to the village at Alarcon—just dip the water you need out of the river and wait in the harbour. If, for some reason, you are not there in time to rendezvous with us Sunday morning, you are to water when and where you can and head for Cornwall without stopping at any Moslem ports between here and Lisbon, and that includes Palma."

Three days later, we rendezvous at the mouth of the Alarcon and I give the captains their orders for our first target—nearby Moorish Almeria and all the transports and galleys in its harbour.

Almeria is a major Moslem port on the Spanish coast and tomorrow we're going to do our usual—row in as if we own the place and cut out all the Moslem galleys and transports we can safely take away. Afterwards, our galleys and their prizes will rendezvous back here to the mouth of the Alarcon River to transfer food and water skins to our prizes.

After we rendezvous, the prizes will row for Crete and then on to Malta and Cyprus. Our fleet of galleys, on the other hand, will head west into the Atlantic and rendezvous again at the mouth of the River Taquin to take on more water and get their new assignments.

******

It was quiet and it stayed quiet as we rowed into Almeria in the scorching hot sun of the early afternoon. It was as if the place was deserted. We quickly seized the only galley we found with slaves on its rowing benches and towed out the three cogs.

There are two other galleys in the harbour without slaves. It would take too many of our men to man their rowing benches so the fire bundles were quickly lit to burn them both. The only conflict was between two of our crews—they both boarded the prize galley at the same time and almost come to blows over whose prize it was.

Before we left, one of our galley captains shouted something over the water and Harold ordered our rudder men to steer closer so we can hear. It was Phillip. He found a possible prize with no slaves on its rowing benches. Instead of burning it, he wants permission to tow it out and let a few of his sailors try to get the empty galley to Cyprus using its sail.

I shouted back my agreement—so long as the men are volunteers and no archers go with them.

I agreed on the condition all the men are volunteers and no archers are involved—because I fear we'll need every one of our archers later and sailing a galley so far without rowers sounds too much like a forlorn hope.

Phillip gave an emphatic nod of his head and raised his thumb to signal his agreement.

A few minutes later a thought hits me—I hope Phillip and his volunteers remembered to check the galley's water supply before they cast off the tow line; with such a small crew, it is unlikely they'll be able to sail their prize into a river mouth or anchor someplace to take on water.

******

Our next rendezvous was a great distance away—

the mouth of an obscure Spanish river running into the Atlantic, the Taquin. Our captains and their pilots were given a week to get their galleys there and join us. They should be able to find it as it is just past the first Moorish city one comes to on Spain's Atlantic coast after passing Gibraltar. They'll turn right and head up the Atlantic coast to it after they go past the big castle which looks down at the narrow gap where the Mediterranean opens into the Atlantic.

Chapter Twenty
The coast of Spain

We sailed in weather that was placid and extremely warm. Or perhaps I should say we rowed in hot weather because the winds were light and infrequent. Even Harold and I took turns on the rowing benches.

It was so hot Helen took to dipping a bucket into the sea and using the water to wash off the sweat which poured off me even when I wasn't rowing; she was a treasure. *It was probably at this moment when I first resolved to change our sailing schedule so we'd spend summers in England and winters on Cyprus.*

It was easy for our galleys to stay together in the placid weather and mirror-like water, and we did. We arrived together at the little inlet at the mouth of the Taquin River and immediately began dipping up water to fill our very depleted water skins.

I hoisted the "captains" flag, and the sergeant captains quickly climbed in their dinghies and rowed to my galley. Even those with a sailor doing the rowing were hot and sweaty when they arrived.

"Well, lads, Almeria was a bust. Let's hope Cadiz has more for us."

There were sharp intakes of breath and soft whistles at my announcement. And then smiles. Cadiz is a great and busy port, perhaps the biggest port in Moslem Spain—and it's one day of easy rowing to the north of here if the weather holds. If we can't take prizes out of Cadiz, we're in the wrong trade.

We'll leave tomorrow in mid-morning so we can hit Cadiz when the day is at its hottest. Then we'll all come back here to make sure our prizes are properly supplied and crewed before we send them on the long and dangerous trip back to Cyprus.

****** *William*

Cadiz was a jewel in the Moslem crown and the principal port on Spain's Moorish Atlantic coast. Its great natural harbour was the home port of a tremendous number of galleys and the centre of the vast fleet of Moorish pirate galleys preying on European shipping. There were rich pickings to be had when the hunters become the hunted, or so we all hoped.

It made no sense to tire our crews, so we rowed easy under the scorching sun and used the sails as much as possible as we moved north along the coast to the harbour entrance. Only our shaded lower rowing benches will be used for rowing until we hurry back out of the harbour with whatever prizes we might take.

We made the turn and entered the harbour entrance with our decks crowded with archers, prize crews, and bales of arrows—both lights and heavies. Then Harold stopped our rowing, and we shaded our eyes against the sun and watched as our nine galleys charged on ahead towards their assigned places. Our assignment was to cover their retreat.

I wasn't about to risk losing all the gold bezants we were carrying in a desperate fight to take one or two more galleys.

Harold and I stood with our hands on the deck railing and watched for almost half an hour as our galleys moved among the transports anchored in the huge harbour and along its three great quays. I was so excited I actually began shivering for a few moments despite the intense heat of the sun.

What we saw was each of our galleys rowing up to an anchored galley, swarming aboard with its boarders and a prize crew to kill everyone they find who wasn't at a rowing bench, and then re-boarding their galley to go on to the next galley—leaving only the men of their prize crew behind to get their new prize underway.

"So far, they all seem to be obeying orders and going for the galleys," I commented quite unnecessarily to Harold who obviously could see what was happening for himself.

I'd made much of going for galleys as prizes because those are what we most need for our own use. As I had explained to our sergeant captains, cogs and other cargo transports may have to be towed out of the harbour to catch the wind; and once you're towing something out of the harbour, it will be hard for you to take another prize—so get any transports last on your way out and, whatever you do, don't get greedy and risk losing your galley and the chest of coins you are carrying.

"Aye, and look there by yon quay, William. Ralph is going after that string of galleys tied side by side; he looks to be trying to take them all, by God."

"Good on him, by God. Good on him. Damn, I hope they all have their slaves on board to row them. He and his men will be rich, by God."

It was very exciting. It was so exciting I motioned Helen to come out from where she was trying peer out of the forward cabin door to see what was happening. She darted her way through all the men and arrow baskets and ran to me with her eyes bright with excitement and breathing heavily.

Within what seems like only a few seconds, the first of our prizes began to be rowed out of the harbour past us with great shouts and waves from the men around us. Others soon followed.

"By God, William, this is much better than Almeria, isn't it?"

"Uh oh. Look over there. A couple of the Moorish galleys have pushed off from the beach and are getting underway."

"Damn, you're right. It's time to go. I'll raise the recall flag and spin us around so we can start moving back towards the entrance."

Seeing our galley moving toward the harbour entrance with the recall flag being waved from our mast was the signal for our captains to quickly finish taking any prizes they've boarded and begin retreating. We'll stay here for a while to cover them and then head for the rendezvous.

******

Two days later, we watched as the last of our prizes got underway for Cyprus via Malta and Crete. Then our ten galleys and their archers began their long run up the Spanish and French coasts and across the Channel to England. It was time to go home.

End of Book Three

Please read more. The rest of the action-packed books in this great saga of medieval England are all available on Kindle as eBooks and some are available in print. You can find them by going to your Amazon website and searching for *Martin Archer fiction*. A collection of the first six books is available on Kindle as *The Archers' Story*. Similarly, a collection of the next four novels in the saga is available as *The Archers' Story: Part II,* and there are additional books beyond those four.

Martin hopes you enjoyed reading *The Archers Return*. If so, he respectfully requests a favourable review on Amazon and elsewhere with as many stars as possible in order to encourage other readers. He can be reached at martinarcherV@gmail.com

Amazon eBooks in the exciting and action-packed *The Company of Archers* saga:

The Archers
The Archers' Castle
The Archer's War
The Archer's Return
Rescuing the Hostages
Kings and Crusaders
The Archers' Gold
The Missing Treasure
Castling the King
The Sea Warriors
The Captain's Men
Gulling the Kings
The Archers' Magna Carta

Amazon eBooks in Martin Archer's exciting and action-packed *Soldier and Marines* saga:

Soldier and Marines
Peace and Conflict
War Breaks Out
War in the East
Israel's Next War

Collections
The Archer's Story - books I, II, III, IV, V, VI

*The Archer's Story II - books VII, VIII, IX, X,
Soldiers and Marines Trilogy*

Other eBooks you might enjoy:
Cage's Crew by Martin Archer writing as Raymond Casey
America's Next War by Michael Cameron

70166073R00107

Made in the USA
Lexington, KY
09 November 2017